The Inn at Holiday Bay:

Clue in the Clam

by

Kathi Daley

The Inn at Holiday Bay

Boxes in the Basement

Letters in the Library

Message in the Mantel

Answers in the Attic

Haunting in the Hallway

Pilgrim in the Parlor

Note in the Nutcracker

Blizzard in the Bay

Proof in the Photo

Gossip in the Garden

Ghost in the Gallery

Turkey in the Trap-Room

Cookies in the Cottage

Details in the Document

Clue in the Clam

Portent in the Pages

Chapter 1

"Welcome to the Inn at Holiday Bay," I greeted the middle-aged man with sandy hair and a sun-kissed tan. "My name is Abby Sullivan. Are you checking in?"

"I am," the man answered. "My name is Christopher Galloway. Please call me Chris."

I looked down at the list my inn manager, Georgia Carter, had left for me. She usually took care of our guests as they checked in and out, but she was away today taping her cable cooking show, *Cooking with Georgia*, so I'd volunteered to hang out at the inn and get everyone checked in so our full-time employee, Jeremy Slater, could continue working on the pond he was building in the yard.

"I see that you've reserved suite five. Will you be staying alone?"

He nodded.

"Did Georgia explain about the stairs?" The inn was laid out over four floors, and unfortunately, we didn't provide an elevator. There was only one suite on the ground floor, so we made sure to let everyone who made a reservation know about the stairs they'd have to travel up and down each day.

"She did, and I'm fine with stairs. In fact, I welcome the extra workout."

It did appear as if the man was in excellent shape physically. If I had to guess, given his bleached hair and tanned skin, I'd say that he worked outdoors.

I asked for a credit card to keep on file. While I ran it, I asked Chris about the reason for his visit. I knew Georgia made a point of getting to know a bit about every guest. Doing so helped the staff create a feeling of family for our visitors during their stay, so I'd decided to do the same.

"I'm a marine biologist. I'm actually in the area to do some research."

"I've always thought the study of marine biology would be interesting. Will you be out on the water?"

"I will. I've rented a boat for the week and will probably be away for the majority of every day. I understand meals are included, so I'll make a point of letting you know which meals I might be here for."

"We'd appreciate that. Having a headcount helps us anticipate quantities needed." I returned the man's credit card and then handed him a key to his suite and a list of events. "I hope you enjoy your week with us and that your research is fruitful."

"Thanks. I appreciate that."

"The suite you're booked into is on the third floor. Once you reach the third-floor landing, take a right. I'll have someone come in and help you with your luggage."

"No need." He picked up his two overnight bags with no problem. "I've got it." He slipped the strap of the smaller bag over his shoulder. "Does the inn provide Wi-Fi?"

"We do. You'll find a binder in your room with all the information you'll need, including a password for the Wi-Fi and a channel lineup for the satellite TV."

His brown eyes flashed with appreciation. "Thanks." He started toward the stairs and then turned back. "Oh, I will be here for dinner this evening. What time do you serve?"

"Cocktails and appetizers are served in the lobby at six, and dinner is served in the dining room at seven. We also offer room service for those who prefer to eat in their suites."

"Good to know. Once I get into my research, I may take advantage of that, but I'll be down tonight. Thanks again."

With that, he headed up the stairs.

We had two other parties checking in today. Jasper and Emma Brown had indicated that they'd be celebrating their fiftieth anniversary while in the area and had booked suite three a year in advance. They were due to arrive this afternoon, so I figured they'd be here at any time.

A woman named Samantha Smith was due to check into suite two within the next hour or two. She'd just given the reason for her stay as rest and relaxation.

Joel Stafford, a retired history professor, who'd been with us the previous month during the storm that hit the area, had taken advantage of a last-minute cancellation and booked suite four. He'd checked in yesterday and would be with us until the following Monday. It was good to see the man who'd helped keep everyone entertained during what had turned out to be a couple of very stressful days.

Also currently checked in was a man named Rodney Kendrick. Apparently, he was an old boyfriend of a Holiday Bay local, Christy Baldwin. According to Georgia, who'd managed to get the scoop during an afternoon event on the lawn, Christy and Rodney had dated all through college, and they'd even discussed marriage, but then Rodney was offered a job overseas. Christy hadn't wanted to move out of the country, so the couple broke up, and Christy eventually married a man named Ron Baldwin. Ron and Christy had a daughter, Haley, but then Ron died, and Christy and Haley moved to Holiday Bay a year and a half ago to be near Ron's parents. Now Christy was engaged to a local church pastor, Noah Daniels, so the fact that Rodney had shown up after all this time was quite interesting.

Suite one was open. A woman named Sydney Whitmore was scheduled to check in tomorrow and stay through the weekend. I was looking forward to her visit since she lived in San Francisco and had known my Ben. I had to admit that I'd been obsessing just a bit about this coincidence ever since she'd called to let me know she'd be in the area and wanted to meet me. Sydney, a forensic psychologist, had been assigned to check out the mass burial site that Georgia and I had uncovered while inspecting a parcel of land I hadn't even known I'd owned until the phone company had made a generous offer to purchase the property. An offer, I was happy to say, I'd accepted since the infusion of cash was going to allow me to build four cottages on the grounds the following summer.

"Welcome to the Inn at Holiday Bay," I greeted a woman who looked to be in her mid-seventies. "My name is Abby Sullivan. You must be Emma Brown."

She smiled, a sort of tired little half-smile, but still a smile. "I am. I have a reservation for a week beginning today."

I looked down at Georgia's notes and nodded. "I have you right here. I see that you're in town with Mr. Brown for your fiftieth anniversary."

The woman's smile faded. "Actually, I'm here alone. My Jasper passed away six months ago."

My hand flew to my heart. I wanted to offer my condolences to Emma, but I sensed it was best to let her finish.

"I probably should have canceled, but to be honest, after Jasper's heart attack, I sort of forgot about it. Then I was looking at my calendar and saw the date and decided to come on my own. I hope that's okay."

"That's perfectly fine. And I'm so very sorry to hear about your husband."

"He lived a long life, and we were happy together for a lot of years. I miss him terribly, but I don't regret a single moment of our time together." She paused for a moment and then continued. "Although I will admit that with all the grief and the disruption to my life since Jasper's death, I haven't had much time to focus on the happy moments in our lives. Once I realized I still had this reservation, I decided to keep it and spend what was to be our fiftieth anniversary remembering."

My heart really did go out to the woman, but I remembered being a new widow and not wanting to deal with outpourings of grief and sorrow from people I barely knew, so I avoided saying more.

"Georgia Carter is the one you spoke to when you booked the room," I said. "She indicated that you wanted to be on the second floor. Is that still the case? We do have the stairs to consider, and the suite on the first floor is currently unoccupied if you want to switch."

"Actually, I think the second floor will be fine. Georgia mentioned that this was an event weekend, and Jasper and I decided that the second floor would be quieter. The stairs shouldn't be a problem."

"Okay then. I just need to run your credit card, and I'll get you settled in."

I realized that Emma had a point about the first floor being noisy during event weekends. It would be nice having other ground floor options once our four cottages were finished.

Once I ran the credit card and grabbed the key, I picked up Emma's luggage without even asking and headed toward the stairs. I was pretty sure Georgia had left a special floral arrangement and bottle of wine for the couple, given their anniversary. I wished I had known about Jasper beforehand so I could have removed them. I hoped that Emma wouldn't find the flowers or wine depressing.

Luckily, she seemed pleased with both, so I set her bags on the floor, showed her where to find the Wi-Fi password and other information she'd need, and then headed back downstairs.

Shortly after I'd returned to the lobby to wait for our last arrival, the landline at the desk rang.

"The Inn at Holiday Bay. This is Abby. How can I help you?"

"Abby. This is Sydney Whitmore."

I smiled. "Sydney. I've been looking forward to meeting you. Are you still planning to arrive tomorrow?"

"Actually, that's why I'm calling. I'm afraid I'm going to have to change my plans. I'm in Virginia, meeting with the forensic team working on identifying the skeletal remains you found. I was planning to head to Holiday Bay tomorrow and stay through the weekend, but I just found out that another victim attributed to the serial killer my team has been trying to track down has been discovered. I'm afraid I need to head back to California right after I inspect the burial site, so my new plan is to fly to Maine tomorrow morning, have a look at the burial site, and then fly back to San Francisco Thursday."

"I'm sorry to hear that, but I do understand."

"Anyway," she continued, "I wanted to let you know about the change in plans in the event you wanted to rebook the room. It seems a waste to save it for me if I'll only be in town one night."

"We're fine with saving it for your use tomorrow. Do you know what time you plan to arrive?"

"Late afternoon; probably between four and five. I plan to head to the burial site first thing and then come by when I'm done there."

"Okay, great. I look forward to meeting you."

It wasn't long after I hung up with Sydney that the last of today's check-ins arrived. Samantha Smith had booked the suite as a single, and it looked as if Georgia had put her into suite two. I asked for her credit card to have on file. The credit card she gave me was assigned to someone named Loretta Long. I asked her about it, and she told me that she was at the inn to get away from it all and was using the name

Samantha Smith although her real name was Loretta Long. It was then that I realized that our guest, who was wearing a dark wig, was actually country-western singer Loretta Long. She asked that I respect her privacy and refer to her as Samantha, and I agreed to do so, but I had to admit that I was curious.

Once everyone was checked in, I decided to head outside to see how Jeremy was doing. The property's extensive landscaping had taken a couple years to install, but for the most part, the hardscape, as well as the majority of the shrubs, trees, and flowerbeds, were in. Jeremy had come to me with the idea of a pond and waterfall feature to be located in one of our shadier areas since most of the grounds didn't feature mature trees to provide shade. I'd loved the idea, but since we hadn't wanted to go to all the trouble of digging a pond and building a waterfall until we knew what we were going to do about the cottages we'd been talking about, we'd had an architect draw up plans that included the pond and waterfall as well as four cottages. The plans also left room for four additional cottages if we decided to go that way at some point down the road.

I hadn't been sure about the cottages in the beginning. The biggest selling point to the suites within the inn was that each one provided an oceanfront view. The way the cottages were tucked in around the property, only one of the four cottages would have a direct ocean view. There was a second cottage with a partial ocean view, but the other two units would be tucked into the gardens near the manmade pond.

The architect had included the landscaping in his drawing, allowing me to see that a cottage near the pond, which would be surrounded by flowers and mature trees, might actually be lovely. I supposed we might have guests who preferred the quiet serenity of the garden rather than a unit with a direct view of the sea.

I'd just arrived at the little path that would take me to the pond when my cell phone rang. "Hey, Georgia," I said after checking the caller ID. "Are you at the house?"

"No, I'm just leaving the studio. I got a call from a man who's apparently connected to the theater company we're using for Saturday's murder mystery. Anyway, he's insisting that we provide photos of the space they will be allotted for the mystery."

"Photos? They want photos of the island?"

"Yes. That's exactly what the guy said they want."

"It's odd that the woman you initially spoke to didn't ask for these photos."

Georgia sighed. "Yes, it is odd. I'm not thrilled with the last-minute request, but I guess I understand why they might want to get a visual of the place. I called and talked to Tanner about using his boat to make a run out to the island this evening, which he was fine with. I spoke to Jeremy, and he assured me that he has dinner covered, so I wanted to see if you and Colt would like to come with us. We can make an evening out of it. Maybe have dinner after I take the photos."

"I'll need to call Colt to confirm that he's available and interested, but I think a trip out to the island sounds fun. What time are you thinking?"

"Tanner is going to meet us at the marina at five-thirty. I'm on my way home now. I'll go over everything with Jeremy before we leave."

"Sounds perfect. I'll talk to you when you get here."

After I hung up with Georgia, I called Colt, who confirmed that he'd enjoy a boat ride and dinner out. He needed to run home and change out of his uniform when he got off, so he said he'd meet us at the marina. Deciding to continue down the path and check in with Jeremy as I'd planned, I headed in that direction.

"Wow. You've really made a lot of progress," I said once I'd arrived at the spot Jeremy had chosen to dig.

"I borrowed the little tractor from the rental place in town, which helped me dig the main body of the pond. Right now, I'm making shelves within the pond for the water plants as well as the step down for the little stream that will feed the waterfall." He wiped the sweat from his brow with the back of his arm. "Did you get everyone checked in okay?"

"I did. It seems like we have a fun group this week. I just spoke to Georgia. I guess she called and spoke to you about dinner."

"She did. I'm going to wrap it up here and then head in to take a shower. Mylie is going to come by around five to help me serve."

"It's nice of Mylie to pitch in the way she does. I almost feel like she should be on the payroll."

He wiped his muddy hands down the legs of his pants. "Mylie doesn't really need the income, and she likes to help out. She says it makes her feel like part of the family. Lately, she's been looking for any excuse to spend time away from the Christy and Noah drama."

"Boy, do I understand that. I feel like things have gone from bad to worse ever since Rodney arrived."

Jeremy shook his head. "Mylie said it's really getting bad. First, Noah and Christy were fighting over the wedding and the growing divide between them about the type of ceremony they wanted to have, and then Rodney shows up and announces that he's moved back to the States and wants to pick things up with Christy where they left off."

"That's ridiculous. Christy has been married and had a child since they dated. She became a widow, fell in love again, and is engaged to Noah now. The fact that this guy thinks he can just swoop in at the eleventh hour is sort of frustrating."

"Yeah," Jeremy agreed. "Mylie has tried to talk to Christy about things, but if she thinks someone is trying to pressure her to do one thing over the other or make any decisions, the harder she seems to push back. I think there's a long history of being dominated in her past, and if you ask my opinion, I think she's over it. I hope she can work things out with Noah, but I honestly won't be surprised if she doesn't."

"You don't think she'd actually give Rodney another chance, do you?" I asked.

Jeremy shrugged. "I wouldn't think so, but I guess you never know what a person is thinking. By the way, I know this is off topic, but I keep trying to remember to ask you if you picked out the flowers that we're going to add to pots on the patio for this weekend. I thought I'd stop by the nursery the first thing in the morning and pick them up. I'd like to get them planted, so any shock they undergo from the replanting will be corrected by the time Friday rolls around."

"I actually went by and picked them out this morning. The nursery is going to deliver the flowers this afternoon. I don't think they planned to be by until later in the day. I'll just have them stack the pallets near the garden shed, and you can get everything planted tomorrow."

"Sounds good. What colors did you go with?"

"Blue and white. I think it will be simple, yet really pretty."

"I agree. Blue and white will be simple, yet nice."

After I wrapped up my conversation with Jeremy, I headed toward the cottage to get ready for the evening. Once I'd showered, I dug around in my closet for something to wear. It might be chilly on the water, especially once the sun set, so I figured I should wear capris rather than shorts and tennis shoes rather than sandals. I added a blue and white short-sleeved top to my dark blue capris and white tennis shoes, and then I grabbed a white zip-up sweatshirt should I need it.

Once I was ready, I looked toward the two dogs and one giant cat, who were watching me. "I suppose I should take you all out."

Ramos turned and headed directly toward the front door as if to let me know that letting him out was an excellent idea. After exiting the cottage from the door leading to the front walkway, I took the path to the right that led to the bluff rather than the one to the left leading to the inn. By the time we got back to the cottage, Georgia had returned from the studio and was getting ready in her bathroom. I had to admit that with the bright sunshine and calm sea, I was really looking forward to tonight's errand, even if I was somewhat annoyed by the last-minute request. We'd booked the actors for the murder mystery months ago, and while we'd only changed the venue from the inn to the island a little over a month ago, if the company needed photos of the space, you'd think they would have asked for them before this.

Chapter 2

The ride across the calm sea to the island was fun. Tanner's boat was fast and sleek, and it seemed to glide effortlessly over the still summer water. Tanner drove, so Georgia sat near him at the center of the vessel while Colt and I cuddled up on the bench seat that ran across the back. We were fortunate that not only was it a calm day, but it was a warm day as well, although even in the direct sun, it wasn't too hot.

A man named Belmont Salinger owned the island we were heading toward. Salinger had purchased the island with the idea of renting it out to groups looking for a private setting for an event or party. The island was uninhabited, although Salinger had put in upgrades such as a sturdy deep water dock, composting toilets, a fire pit with benches, and a flat area sufficient in size to set up the long tables and plastic chairs which were kept stored on the island.

Salinger also sent a maintenance crew out to the island after every event, which we really appreciated since it appeared the island was as pristine as we'd been promised it would be.

When we arrived at the island, Tanner tied up, and we all climbed out onto the dock. The main drawback I saw was that there wasn't a lot of natural shade on the island. I assumed one of the reasons no one had ever built a home or resort on the island was due to the lack of fresh water.

"Those large metal buildings you see in the distance house tables, chairs, grills, and other supplies," Georgia said. "On Saturday morning, Jeremy and I plan to meet the two men provided by Salinger. The two men will stick around to make sure the equipment is being treated with respect and to answer any questions or deal with any problems that may arise."

"And the food?" I asked.

"Tanner is going to pick up Mylie and Nikki, who are going to bring it over closer to event time. We'll be dependent on ice chests since there isn't any electricity on the island."

"So will there be tiki torches and a bonfire for light once it gets dark?"

"We shouldn't have to deal with the darkness, but we do plan to provide both for atmosphere."

"And what are the arrival and departure times for the boats ferrying the guests?" I asked.

"The first boat will drop guests off on the island at four o'clock, and I think we should have all fifty guests ferried over by five. The theater company will explain the setup for the murder mystery while drinks and appetizers are served buffet style. Once the rules and the setup are explained, the guests will divide into teams and then begin the process of following the clues that will be provided in plastic clams. During this time, the guests will be free to mingle so they can ask each other questions and that sort of thing."

"Will our staff need to do anything during that portion of the evening?" I wondered.

"No. The theater company will run the mystery. Jeremy and I will prepare the meal during that time, and Nikki and Mylie will manage the drinks and appetizers. We plan to sit down for dinner around seven. The theater group plans to wrap up the mystery during the meal, and the first ferry back to the marina will leave at eight-thirty. We hope to have everyone back to the marina by nine-thirty. Tanner and his buddy, Harold, are both bringing their boats, so our group should be able to head back with them."

"And what about the meal itself?" I asked.

"In addition to clams, I have lobster, shrimp, scallops, crab, corn cobs, and potatoes. I also have plenty of salads and desserts."

"It sounds like you've thought of everything," I acknowledged.

"I hope so. We're not going to be able to run into town if we find we've forgotten something. It's a risk having the event on the island rather than at the inn, but if we pull this off, I think that it's going to be the sort of thing folks talk about for years to come."

"At least the weather forecast looks to be just about perfect," Colt said. "I was somewhat concerned it would rain when I first heard your plan."

"Don't even say that," Georgia paled. "I need to take some photos for the theater company members who have little skits to act out. I'll need about thirty minutes if the rest of you want to wander around."

During the wandering around portion of our evening, I stumbled across the last thing I wanted to find.

"Is that...?" I asked.

"Oliver Halifax," Colt said as he jogged forward and knelt down in the sand next to the very dead body of the local town councilman.

Chapter 3

After we'd found Oliver's body the previous afternoon, Colt had called his office and requested that both the coroner and one of his deputies come out to the island to see to the removal of the body. Tanner had brought Georgia and me back to the cottage, where I made a sandwich, and Georgia grabbed her dog and an overnight bag to take to Tanner's. Colt had promised to call when he found out more about what was going on, but he never did. I supposed I'd call him for an update this morning.

Once the coffee had brewed, I settled onto the sofa with my dog, Molly, and my cat, Rufus. I hated waking to an alarm, so I enjoyed the quiet when I happened to naturally wake before dawn. As the first hint of daylight appeared on the horizon, I refilled my coffee, grabbed a blanket, and took both animals out onto my private deck overlooking the sea.

Unless Georgia had made arrangements with Jeremy to handle breakfast, which I imagined she might have, I supposed she would be home soon. Jeremy and Georgia worked well together, each giving the other needed breaks and vacation time. Georgia and I both felt that we'd really lucked out that he'd chosen our inn to stay at when he'd come to the area looking for a job shortly after we'd opened.

"Morning, Abby," Georgia poked her head out the sliding glass door. "You're up early."

"I couldn't sleep, so I decided to watch the sunrise." I held up my mug. "There's coffee if you have time."

"I have time. Tanner had a class, so he dropped me off early. I'll just grab a mug and be right back."

By the time Georgia returned and settled onto the lounger next to me, the sky had just begun to turn a deep red. Ramos and Molly greeted each other by running around in circles on the sand while Rufus watched from the safety of a lounge chair.

"Have you spoken to Colt?" Georgia asked.

"Not yet, but I do plan to call him."

"Tanner called and spoke to Colt early this morning," she informed me. "They spoke for quite a while, and while I didn't hear everything that was said, Tanner did mention that Colt had shared that the coroner found a little plastic clam between Oliver's hands which no one had noticed until after the coroner had taken a closer look."

"Do you mean a plastic clam like the ones the theater company plans to use for the murder mystery?"

"Exactly like that. Like the clams used for the mystery, the clam found in Halifax's hand opened. A piece of paper which simply said greed was inside the clam."

"Greed?" I asked. "That's it?"

Georgia nodded.

"What on earth could that mean?"

"I'm not sure. Tanner wasn't sure either, but he did point out that the term greed seems to fit. Oliver Halifax seemed to have a hunger for money, and he was greedy for attention. He liked to be in the center of whatever is going on, and he'd run for and was elected to the town council recently. His entry into the race was a last-minute decision that seemed to have come from out of nowhere. Most people thought that he didn't have a chance since the incumbent had been campaigning for months, and when he won, the rumors started circulating that he'd cheated."

"Did he cheat?" I wondered.

Georgia shrugged. "Tanner wasn't sure. He did say that there was evidence to back up the claim of those who say he did."

I didn't know Oliver Halifax well, but I knew who he was. He was rich, successful, and good-looking. I seemed to remember hearing that he had a wife but couldn't say that I'd ever met her. If I remembered correctly, Oliver Halifax was some sort of investment broker and a very successful one at that. "Do you know why Oliver even wanted to be on the town council?" I asked. "He seemed like the sort of guy who was already pretty busy."

Georgia took a sip of her coffee. "Tanner mentioned that Oliver seemed most interested in the new resort proposed for the coastline south of town."

I'd heard about the project. The proposed mega-resort was causing a lot of controversy in town since there were men and women with strong opinions on both sides of the issue. Those in support of the project argued that the resort would provide lots of jobs and bring a large influx of tourists and tourist dollars to the area, but it was also the sort of commercial project a lot of the old-timers didn't want to see get a foothold.

"I know that both Ellington Simpleton and Councilman Covington favor approval of the project," I commented. "I've also heard that Evelyn Child and Sonya Greenly are against the development of the area. So I guess the deciding vote would have come down to Oliver Halifax if he hadn't died. Do you know how he planned to vote?"

"I don't. Tanner didn't know either, but he did say that Oliver thrived on being in the hot seat. The guy was the sort who only seemed to be happy when all eyes were on him, which is why Tanner thinks he challenged the incumbent, Dennis Painter, for his seat on the council once he realized that it would be Dennis who had the deciding vote."

Talk about a crazy reason to run for an elected position.

"Do you think it's possible that someone knew how Oliver planned to vote and killed him in order to prevent that vote from happening?"

Georgia frowned. "Maybe. The resort is a mega-million dollar project, and if it's approved, it will completely change the atmosphere of our quaint little seaside town. I've heard that emotions are high on both sides. Like I've said before, it's complicated."

I'd hate to think that anyone would kill a man over property development, but as Georgia had said, emotions were high, so maybe. "Did Colt mention the cause of death to Tanner?"

She nodded. "The medical examiner told Colt that the man was given a lethal injection which would have stopped his heart almost immediately. It appeared as if he'd been killed elsewhere and then taken to the island where the body was staged."

I thought back and tried to remember what I'd seen. The man had been lying on his side. His legs had been bent, and his arms were resting one against another as if he'd been sleeping. I hadn't noticed any blood. It really did look as if the man had simply drifted off.

"So someone gave this man a lethal injection, moved him out to the island, and posed his remains to make it appear as if he was simply sleeping. Why go to so much trouble to do things exactly that way?"

Georgia shrugged. "Colt didn't know." She looked at her watch. "I need to head inside and jump in the shower. I have the breakfast prep done, but I still need to put everything together."

"I'm going to sit out here for a few more minutes, and then I'll get ready as well. I thought I'd take the opportunity to get to know some of the guests who've checked in this week a bit better. Oh, and I wanted to remind you that Sydney Whitmore will be arriving later this afternoon. I'd really like to have a chance to talk to her one on one, so perhaps we can have our dinner here on the deck."

"I think that sounds like a good idea. I'll have a private meal ready for you at six so you can talk without the others listening in. I'm looking forward to meeting this woman. I wouldn't want to do what she does, but it is fascinating."

"I agree. I'm sorry it didn't work out for Sydney to stay longer, but I understand that she has a demanding job. Can you imagine having a job where you're on the East Coast doing research involving one serial killer only to be called back to the West Coast early due to the activity of another serial killer?"

"Can I imagine that? No, I can't, but I suspect there are those who thrive in that sort of environment. Should we try to fill the room for the weekend since she won't be staying?"

"No, let's just leave it vacant. I called Lacy after Sydney called me, hoping that Lonnie and Lacy could work something out for at least one night, but Lacy wasn't comfortable leaving the kids for so long while they were sick." Lonnie and Lacy had planned to spend time with us at the inn while her parents took their six children to Florida for two weeks, but the twins had gotten sick at the last minute, so they'd canceled their reservation, and we'd booked their room to Joel Stanford. When Sydney called to say she wouldn't be using the room for the entire week, I'd hoped Lonnie and Lacy could make it work for a shorter stay, so I'd called Lacy about the vacancy. "I really do feel bad for everyone involved. I told Lacy that we'd find a place to slip her and Lonny in another time if she can get a sitter. Maybe they can manage a long weekend. If not during the summer, then maybe in the fall."

"I heard that Mary might have to have her tonsils out."

I nodded. "Lacy mentioned that while both girls were sick, Mary seems to be the one who's sick more often, and her pediatrician is looking at options."

Georgia headed inside, and I finished watching the day awaken. It was mornings like this when I knew in my soul that no matter what the future might bring, there was nowhere in the world I'd rather be.

Chapter 4

Once I'd showered and dressed, I headed over to the inn to say hi to our guests. Sydney wasn't due to arrive for hours, so I supposed once I'd done that, I'd head into town and take care of a few errands. I knew if I didn't stay busy, the waiting was going to drive me crazy.

By the time I made it to the inn, Emma was sitting on the patio sipping a cup of coffee. I knew she was here to spend time with her memories and hated to disturb her, but she waved at me, so I waved back and headed in her direction.

"It's a beautiful morning," I said.

She smiled softly. "It really is. My Jasper would have loved sitting out here listening to the sound of the waves as the new day dawned. You really do have the perfect spot to while away a summer morning."

"I have to say that I agree with you about that." I motioned to a chair at the table she sat at. "May I?"

"Please."

I sat down. "So, how has your trip been so far?" I thought it best not to dwell on the fact that it had to be depressing to take your fiftieth-anniversary trip alone.

"It's actually been lovely. I went into town with Joel and Samantha yesterday. We did some shopping and then had a delicious lunch. Joel shared the story of his first trip to your inn during the storm last month. He made it sound both exciting and a bit horrifying."

"I suppose both are true. Joel actually helped quite a lot. He kept other guests busy in the library during the worst of it. I think his efforts helped calm everyone's nerves."

"The man has an interesting past. He's traveled extensively, and he knows a lot about many things. He kept Samantha and me laughing all through lunch. I know I appreciated the effort to distract me on what could have been a very difficult day, and I could sense that Samantha was relieved to have a diversion as well." Emma leaned forward a bit. "She didn't say as much, but I think Samantha is here to deal with her own loss. There's something in her eyes that I recognize."

"Yes, I had the same impression. I think it's nice that the three of you have spent some time together. And Joel really is great."

"The three of us are going to take a drive down to the national park today. I hear the scenery is spectacular."

"It really is," I agreed. "There are drives you can take and some outstanding hikes if you're feeling a bit more energetic."

"I'm not sure I'm up for much of a hike, but a drive sounds lovely. I understand there are some breathtaking views from within the park boundaries."

"There really are. And the visitor center is worth stopping to visit as well. Have you traveled in this area before?"

"No. My Jasper always wanted to visit Maine, but somehow we never made the trip. When we started talking about a big trip for our anniversary, I knew I wanted to bring him here." She paused. A faraway look crossed her face. "In a way, it feels wrong to be here without him, but I gave it a lot of thought and realized that he'd want me to enjoy the scenery for both of us."

"I'm sure you're right." I offered the woman a smile.

I chatted with Emma for a few more minutes and then headed inside. After entering through the back door, I poked my head into the dining area and then wandered back into the kitchen where Georgia was preparing the morning meal. "It looks like the dining room is empty. Emma must be the only one up."

"Actually, Chris is up and gone. I doubt he'll be back until dinner. Maybe not even then. He indicated he'd text me later. I haven't seen Samantha or Rodney yet, but Joel is in the library."

I picked up a muffin and tore off an edge. "Emma told me that she has plans with Samantha and Joel to go to the national park today. It sounded like they'd be away most of the day. It looks like we should have an empty inn between breakfast and dinner, assuming that Rodney has plans as well."

Georgia frowned. "When I spoke to him yesterday, he mentioned that Christy and Haley planned to give him the grand tour today. I know we're supposed to be friendly and helpful toward all our guests, but I'm having a hard time liking the guy."

"I know what you mean. It feels wrong that the man is here to steal Noah's fiancée away from him, but the reality is that the only way he has a shot at stealing Christy is if the issues between Christy and Noah are so great as to create an opportunity for Rodney to swoop in. If that's true, if Christy and Noah have found themselves with an unresolvable rift, then it's best to figure that out before they walk down the aisle."

Georgia opened the oven and rearranged things a bit. "Yeah, I guess that's true. Mylie is really upset about the whole thing, but Jeremy responded to her concern with a comment similar to what you just said.

I guess if Christy doesn't choose Noah, then maybe her not choosing him is something that would have happened down the line anyway." Georgia slid a tray of biscuits into the second of our two wall ovens. "I do think that it's Noah's mother who's created all the problems, but I get why Christy is hesitant to marry a man who doesn't seem to be willing to put her wishes over those of his mother. Christy has mentioned on occasion that Haley's father was completely under the thumb of his domineering mother and that it put a strain on things. I can see how that sort of pattern will only lead to trouble down the road." Georgia set out pitchers of orange and grapefruit juice. "Maybe Rodney is the test the relationship Noah and Christy have established needs to withstand if the couple has any chance at all."

"Maybe," I agreed, picking up the juice and heading to the dining room where breakfast was being set up buffet style on the sideboard. "I have a bunch of errands to do in town before Sydney arrives. Do you need anything?"

Georgia picked up a platter with meat and another with potatoes and carried them to the dining room, so I grabbed the bowl of scrambled eggs and followed her.

"Actually, would you mind stopping at the seafood market down at the marina? I need to pay for the clams I have on order for Saturday, and I've been promised the catch of the day if I pay a deposit and reserve the fish I'm planning to grill for dinner tomorrow night today."

"Yeah. No problem. I guess we'll need to pick the catch of the day up tomorrow."

"I've made arrangements to have it delivered. There was an extra charge, but I figured it would save us some time. I've spoken to the guests, and everyone is in for a cookout on the back patio. In addition to the fish, I'm going to grill veggies and provide a couple different salads."

"Sounds fun and delicious. Is there anything else you need?"

"Actually," Georgia began, "if you have time and don't mind stopping by the farmers market, it will save me time tomorrow if you want to pick up the veggies today."

"I'd be happy to. Just make me a list."

Once breakfast had been set out, I chatted with the guests who'd come down for the meal and then headed back to the cottage. I decided to make a list of stops so I didn't forget anything. I needed to stop by the bookstore to sign a stack of books the bookstore's owner planned to use as part of a promotion, and then I needed to go to the bank and the dry cleaners. In addition to stopping at the seafood market to pay for the clams and put a deposit down for tomorrow's catch of the day, Georgia had asked me to stop at the farmers market to buy a variety of vegetables. Additionally, I wanted to stop and chat with Colt, so I supposed I should get going if I wanted to be back by the time Sydney arrived.

My first stop was Firehouse Books. The owner, Vanessa Blackstone, seemed to be even more excited about promoting my books than I was. It's not that that I wasn't excited, but Vanessa was the one who was always coming up with new and unique ways to catch the interest of potential readers.

"Good morning, Vanessa," I greeted. "I'm here to sign the books for the promotion."

"Oh good. Did you remember bookmarks?"

I held up a box.

"Wonderful. There's already been a lot of interest in the signature collection, and I'm sure you'll be pleased to know that of all the authors who are taking part, your books are among the most popular."

I smiled. "You know I'm always happy to log a sale."

Vanessa opened the box with the bookmarks and began to organize them into stacks. I had to say that the friendly bookstore owner was both hardworking and organized. I noticed a table featuring mysteries and romances set along the coast of Maine. The display was creatively outfitted with fishing nets and plastic clams, much like the ones we were using for the murder mystery.

"It seems like there are a lot of tourists in town for Clam Bake week," I said.

She nodded. "Business has been good. I'm looking forward to the bands that are playing in the gazebo in the park this evening, and I understand there will be craft vendors in the park this weekend as well."

"Georgia has a list of everything that's going on. It did seem extensive. Personally, I've been so busy planning the murder mystery and our clam bake on the island that I haven't paid much attention to anything else."

"Speaking of the murder mystery on the island," Vanessa said. "I heard about Oliver Halifax. I understand that his body was found out on the same island you're planning to use for your event."

"Yes, that was tragic." I decided not to mention the fact that I was with the group who found him. I was interested in hearing what Vanessa had to say, but I didn't want to get into too deep of a conversation since I had so many stops to make.

"I heard that his death might have something to do with the election and his involvement with Vivica Desmond."

I frowned. "I'm not sure I know Vivica Desmond."

"She works as a clerk for the town. The job she was hired for is clerical in nature, doing the filing and that sort of thing. But apparently, if rumor can be believed, Vivica is the one who used her access to town records to help Oliver obtain information on his opponents in the last election. Popular opinion is that without that information, a last-minute candidate like Oliver could never have won." She leaned in a bit. "You know, Dennis Painter is the councilman he beat out. It seems to me that might give Dennis reason to be angry at the man. I'm not sure a lost election is a motive for murder, but maybe. At the very least, I'd look into it."

The idea that Dennis had killed Oliver over the election didn't really jive with the manner in which his body was found or with the note that was left in the clam. Of course, Vanessa didn't know any of that.

I chatted with Vanessa for a while longer and then headed toward the bank. After making a deposit into the account that I used for the inn and my personal account, I took out the cash I'd need for the seafood market and headed toward the cleaners.

"Afternoon, Mr. Manson," I greeted the owner of the establishment. "I'm picking up my dry cleaning." I handed him the claim ticket. He checked the number and began to search for my sweaters.

"There sure are a lot of folks in town this week," I said conversationally.

"We always have a good turnout for Clam Bake week." He hung my order on the rack and then rang me up. "That stain you wanted me to take a look at came out with no problem."

I smiled and handed him my credit card. "That's wonderful news."

He rang up my order and returned my credit card. I reached for the clothes and had just turned to leave when Mrs. Manson walked through the front door.

"Did you hear about Henry Goodman?" she asked without even pausing to acknowledge my presence.

"No. What's Henry up to now?" Mr. Manson asked.

"He's dead," Mrs. Manson answered.

"Dead?" I asked. "Are you sure?" Perhaps the woman was confusing Henry Goodman with Oliver Halifax.

"I'm sure. I was over at the diner talking to Velma when Buck Owens came in."

I knew that Buck owned the hardware store.

"Apparently, someone called Buck earlier in the day to complain about an electrical problem in the gazebo in the park," Mrs. Manson continued. "There's a music event in the gazebo to kick off Clam Bake week this evening, so Buck offered to go over and take a look. When he got there, he found Henry under a tarp. The man was laying on his side as if he was simply sleeping."

"Two murders in two days." Mr. Manson remarked. "Whatever is going on?"

Mrs. Manson wasn't sure, and I wasn't either, but I did intend to find out.

The first thing I did was call Colt's cell, but he didn't answer. I then called his office but was told by his receptionist that he was out on a call. I figured I'd head over to Velma's next. If there was gossip afoot, Velma was usually the first one to hear about it. I called Velma, who told me to come on by. I was close to the marina, so I decided to stop there first. I told Velma I'd be by in about twenty minutes.

I loved the flavor and texture of the fresh fish that they sold the same day they were brought in, but entering the market from the outside provided an olfactory experience I wasn't looking to repeat any more than need be.

"I'm here to pay for the clams and put down the deposit for the fish my inn manager ordered," I said to the tall, brawny man behind the counter.

"Ah. Yes. You must be Abby."

I nodded.

"You do understand that by putting in an order for the catch of the day, you are ordering whatever the men bring in, don't you?"

"I understand. According to Georgia, everything you sell is fresh and delicious, so she was willing to place the order as it is offered."

"Okay. I'll ring it up for you. We only accept cash."

"I brought cash." I pulled my wallet out of my shoulder bag. "I understand that you're going to deliver the catch of the day to the inn tomorrow once the fishermen come in, and you see what you have to offer."

He nodded. "I'll send my son. He can collect the balance."

I handed the man the agreed-upon amount of cash, and he went to work providing a handwritten receipt. Once I said my goodbyes, I headed to Velma's to see what, if anything, she'd heard. Just as

I was pulling up in front of the diner, I received a text from Colt letting me know he'd received my message but would be busy with interviews for the next couple of hours. He promised to call me later, which I supposed would have to do.

When I arrived at the diner, a group at a table by the window was just finishing up. Velma offered me iced tea, which I accepted. She indicated that I should grab a booth back in the corner and that she'd join me once she finished up with her customers. I figured that I wasn't in a hurry, so I did as she suggested, pulling out my cell phone to check my emails while I waited.

There was one from my sister letting me know that a long-time family friend had passed away. It seemed that all the emails from my sister lately had to do with friends or family members who had passed. I supposed Annie wasn't the sort to send a chatty email unless she had something specific to pass on. I also supposed that I'd fallen into that same pattern since moving to Holiday Bay.

There was also an email from my agent letting me know that my publisher had loved both book proposals I'd sent in. I planned to take some time off from writing this summer, but it looked as if I would be busy on that aspect of my life once things slowed down at the inn.

One of my old friends from San Francisco had emailed to let me know that she was moving to Vermont and would look me up once she got settled, and my dentist wanted to remind me that I was overdue for my cleaning.

All in all, a fairly boring set of emails until I got to the last one that is.

"You're frowning," Velma said, sliding into the booth across from me once the last group of customers had left.

"I just received an email from the young woman who caused the accident that killed Ben and Johnathan." I looked across the table. "I guess I told you that she walked into the police station and turned herself in after all these years. Someone from the DA's office called me a month or so ago to inform me of the situation and to get my feedback."

"I remember that. The woman's attorney was trying to work out a plea deal which would allow the woman to avoid prison and keep her baby."

I nodded. "The woman just wanted to let me know that everything worked out and that she was so very sorry for her actions three and a half years ago that led to the death of my family. She assures me that her life was forever changed at that moment and that she will live the rest of her life trying to make amends for her actions."

"How did this woman get your email?" Velma asked.

"It's actually on my webpage."

"Ah. I guess I can understand that. I forget that in addition to being Abby from Holiday Bay, you're also Abagail Sullivan, the award-winning author." She glanced at the cell phone in my hand. "Does she say anything else?"

"She said that she recently inherited a significant amount of money from her grandmother that she plans to donate to the local children's hospital in Johnathan's memory. She assures me that she doesn't want anything from me and that I don't even need to reply to the email. She said that she just wanted to be sure I understood the depth of her sorrow over what occurred."

Velma sat back in the booth. "So does all that make you feel better or worse?"

I narrowed my gaze. "I'm actually not sure. I guess I'm glad that the woman really is sorry that her actions led to the deaths of a really good man and his infant son. But her being sorry doesn't bring them back. On the one hand, the email brought up a horrific event I would just as soon not have been reminded of." I set my cell phone down on the table. "On the other hand, I do appreciate that the woman was a child who did nothing worse than suffer a lapse in judgment more than three years ago. This lapse in judgment resulted in a horrific tragedy, which she then chose not to own up to, but I don't think that necessarily makes her a bad person. Truth be told, I've glanced down to check a text while driving a time or two as well."

"It does seem like she really is trying to do the right thing at this point," Velma offered.

I nodded. "It does." I took a sip of my iced tea. "I'm actually here to talk about Henry Goodman. I just heard that his body was found in the gazebo in the park."

She nodded. "I don't know a lot, but I do know that Buck found him when he went to look at an electrical problem. Apparently, if the rumors are accurate, he was found lying on his side just like Oliver Halifax, and just like Oliver, he had a plastic clam between his hands."

"Do you know if there was a note inside the clam?"

She shrugged. "Buck didn't touch anything, so I'm not sure. He found the body and called Colt. If Buck hadn't been notified about the electrical problem and headed over to check it out, the odds are that the body would have been discovered this evening when half the town was there for the event."

I frowned. "Did Buck say who called him about the electrical problem?"

She slowly moved her head from left to right. "No, I don't think he said."

"It seems odd that Georgia was called yesterday by someone who told her that he worked for the theater company and needed photos of the island. When we arrived, we found Oliver's body. Then today, Buck is called about an electrical problem in the gazebo, and when he gets there, he finds victim number two."

"Do you think the calls were intended to make sure that someone found the bodies?"

"Maybe. I guess we'll have to find out who called Buck. If it turns out that the same person who called

Georgia also called Buck, then I'd say the calls and deaths are probably related."

"I think the deaths have to be related in some way," Velma agreed. "Both men had a political connection of sorts with the town, and both men were linked to that new development. I know that Goodman was working with the developer to get all the permits approved and processed. Based on what I've been able to find out, Oliver Halifax was in a position of breaking any tie over the proposition before the town to allow that developer to build the monstrosity of a resort he's trying to build." Velma paused and continued. "If my research is correct, William Covington and Ellington Simpleton are both pro-development, while Evelyn Child and Sonya Greenly are both against any sort of development that will drastically change the landscape of our small town. That means Oliver Halifax would have been the tiebreaker."

Velma was the second person to mention this. Maybe the proposed resort and the local election were behind all of this after all.

Chapter 5

By the time I arrived home, it was after three, and Sydney had indicated that she planned to arrive between four and five. Deciding I had time to wash off the dust and fish smell from the day, I headed toward the shower. As I shampooed my hair, I considered what to wear for my dinner with our special guest. It was sort of odd that I was feeling nervous about meeting this woman. I wasn't sure why exactly. She seemed really nice, but she had known Ben, and he'd never mentioned her, so I guessed the whole thing left me feeling off my game a bit. As I rinsed my hair, I thought back to our first conversation. Sydney had shared that she'd worked with Ezra Reinhold a few times, which was how she knew Ben. Ezra Reinhold was a reclusive billionaire who had lived in San Francisco at one time but had retired to a large estate on the very north end of

Shipwreck Island after a home invasion had resulted in the death of his wife and son.

I remembered that Ben had mentioned him on many occasions, so I supposed it made sense that Ben had gone to him if he needed help with one of the cold cases he liked to work on. Ezra never left his estate, but he did employ a large staff as well as a civilian crime-fighting team Ben had referred to as a real-life Justice League.

Turning the water off, I wrapped a towel around my body and stepped out of the shower. I supposed I should wear something casual but not too casual for our dinner. The woman worked for the FBI, so chances were that she might show up in a black suit of some sort.

As I dried my hair, I thought about the information Colt had dug up. Apparently, there was reason to believe that the bones Georgia and I had found on a parcel of land I owned belonged to victims of Grover McClellan, a serial killer currently incarcerated in California for a string of deaths on the West Coast. McClellan was claiming that he'd also been responsible for a string of deaths on the East Coast years ago and that the bones we'd found belonged to bodies he'd buried there. When we'd spoken, Sydney indicated that it was her job to try to separate fact from fiction.

Deciding on yellow capris, white sandals, and a flowery top, I headed to my closet. I hoped nothing came up which would prevent Sydney from showing up since, by this point, my curiosity about the woman had shifted into overdrive.

Luckily, only minutes after I finished applying a light coat of makeup to my tanned face and walked to the inn, I heard a car in the drive.

"Sydney?" I greeted after opening the door and stepping out onto the drive. The woman was dressed in dusty jeans with a black t-shirt tucked into the waistband. She had dirty tennis shoes on her feet and a streak of mud on her cheek. I had to admit she wasn't at all what I was expecting.

"That's me." The petite woman with long blond hair and blue eyes, who looked a lot like Georgia, smiled as she got out of the blue sedan she'd been driving. "I'm afraid I'm a bit of a mess after digging around in the dirt all afternoon." She reached into the car and took out a bag. "Is there a place I can change into something clean?"

"Absolutely," I stepped aside, inviting the woman in. "I have your suite ready for you. I'll just show you in. Do you have luggage?"

"Just one bag." She held up a small travel bag.

After I introduced Sydney to Georgia, who was busy in the kitchen, I escorted her to suite one, letting her know that I'd be waiting in the cottage and that she should just come on over whenever she was ready. She indicated that she needed to shower and change and call her boss, so perhaps she'd meet me there in an hour. I assured her that an hour was fine and that I was anxious to get to know her.

Sixty minutes later, Sydney showed up wearing dark blue shorts and a light blue top. She wore sandals, and she'd pulled her long hair into a braid that trailed down her back. "Thank you. I feel better. I didn't realize there would be so much mud."

"We've had some rain lately. You were smart to wear jeans to the site."

"Experience has taught me to be prepared." She bent down to pet Rufus, who'd wandered up to say hi. Georgia had the dogs with her at the inn.

I suggested we talk out on the deck and offered her a beverage. She chose a glass of white wine, which sounded good to me as well. Georgia had made us plates that were warming in the oven, but we'd decided to start with a fruit and cheese tray and then segue into the main course after we'd had a chance to chat for a while.

Once we were settled with our appetizers, we chatted about the view, the inn, and Sydney's trip to the East Coast. I was really most interested in her work and the bones that had brought her here in the first place, as well as her association with Ben, but decided it was best to ease into those subjects.

"So what exactly does a forensic psychologist do?" I asked after the subjects of the inn and the weather had been exhausted.

Sydney leaned back in her chair. "Actually, the term forensic psychologist is a general term that applies to any psychologist who works in the criminal justice system. Some forensic psychologists do evaluations, both in child custody cases and in criminal litigation. Other psychologists work with attorneys to aid in jury selection, and others might work with witnesses before they testify. Some psychologists provide counseling to inmates, while others work in the areas of rehabilitation and reintegration into society after release. I decided to go into profiling."

"Is that something you always wanted to do?"

"Not at all. Initially, I was interested in counseling in the private sector. I planned to obtain my doctorate and then open my own practice, but I did a summer internship at a prison while working on my doctorate. I guess you can say that experience changed me because by the time summer was over, I had realized I was fascinated with the criminal mind, so I applied for and was accepted into the FBI profiling program. I worked with a team on the East Coast for a while, but my family is in California, so when the opportunity to work out of the San Francisco office presented itself, I jumped on it."

"And do you like what you do?"

She hesitated. "My job can be mentally and emotionally challenging, but I feel that what I do is worthwhile."

I realized that she hadn't actually said that she liked her job, only that she found it worthwhile. If I knew Sydney a bit better, I might dig around in her obvious attempt to divert the answer, but I didn't know her all that well, and it really wasn't any of my business.

"So did you meet Ben while working for the FBI office in San Francisco?" I asked, changing the subject.

She paused and then answered. "Yes and no. Ben and I met after I started working out of the San Francisco office, but we actually met on Shipwreck Island. Did Ben mention a man named Ezra Reinhold to you?"

I nodded. "Ezra is a tech billionaire with a tragic past who decided to seclude himself in a private estate on an island where he sponsors a team of civilians who fight crime."

"Basically yes, although, don't be fooled by the term civilian. Ezra employs the best money can buy. I was first introduced to Ezra by a woman I met while working on the East Coast. Octavia is ex-CIA, and our paths had crossed a time or two."

"Why did she quit the CIA to go to work for Ezra?"

She shrugged. "I think Octavia became disillusioned along the way with some of the protocols she'd been forced to adhere to."

"So Ezra is a rule breaker?"

"If breaking the rules will achieve the desired outcome." She took a sip of her wine. "Anyway, as I said, I met Octavia when she was still with the CIA, but we stayed in touch even after she decided to work for Ezra. I was home visiting family on Shipwreck Island when I ran into Octavia. We got to talking, and she invited me to a strategy session the group was holding that evening. It was then and there that I first met the team. After I moved to California, I was asked to join in from time to time. I happened to meet

Ben during one of the meetings I'd decided to attend."

"Can you tell me why he'd approached the group?" I had to admit I'd been wondering that since I'd spoken to Sydney on the phone.

"Ben was working on a cold case involving a missing sixteen-year-old. At least she was sixteen when she went missing, but by the point when he brought the case to the group, she would have been nineteen. Anyway, this case wasn't one he was officially working on for the SFPD. I guess you know he liked to poke around in unsolved cases in his spare time."

"Yes, I do know that. Why did Ben think the group could help him on this particular cold case?"

"Honestly, I'm not sure how it is he came to approach the group. What I do know is that Libby Bolinger went missing after attending a movie with friends and was never seen again. Her parents were sure she'd been abducted, but there wasn't any evidence that she had been, so the detective who was looking into the case filed it away as a teen runaway case. Apparently, Ben came across the file and decided to look into it. He knew about Ezra's group, and he somehow managed to get an invite to present the case to the team. That, in and of itself, was quite the feat. Ezra doesn't invite just anyone to his meetings, and he doesn't take on every case that comes his way."

I knew that Ben could be very persuasive. I wasn't at all surprised that he'd talked this man into hearing what he had to say. "So did they find Libby?"

"Actually, they did. It seems that a man named Dugan Dunsmore was a survivalist living with his five sons in Idaho up near the Canadian border. Apparently, when each of his sons turned sixteen, Dugan found them a wife."

"Found them a wife? Are you saying that he kidnapped a wife for his sons?"

"That's exactly what I'm saying. By the time the team managed to track Libby down, she was nineteen and 'married' to the youngest Dunsmore son, who was likewise nineteen at that point. When I say 'married,' I'm not referring to a legal ceremony, but a commitment ceremony that had been forced on them by Dunsmore."

"So what happened after Ezra's team found Libby? Did she go home?"

"Actually, no. When the team showed up to save Libby, she no longer wanted to be saved. She'd fallen in love with the man she'd married, and the couple had a nine-month-old daughter named Star."

"So what happened? Did she stay with her husband in Idaho?"

She nodded. "Yes, she did. It took a while for law enforcement to sort everything out, but the only men who were involved in the actual kidnapping of these women were Dugan and eventually his oldest son, Clive."

"So Dugan kidnapped a sixteen-year-old girl for Clive, and then once Clive was a bit older, he helped his father kidnap the girls for his brothers?"

"Basically, yes. Clive and his wife, Julianna, had four sons by the time everything came to a head. Clive was in on the kidnapping of the girls three of his younger brothers were to marry, so he, along with Dugan, were arrested, and Julianna and her four sons were sent back to Kansas, where she was originally taken from and where her parents still lived. The second son, Cole, was in his mid-twenties by this point, but while he'd been forced by his father to marry the girl picked out for him, apparently, he never consummated the marriage, and the two had lived as friends. Cole and his wife left the compound and settled in LA, where they eventually led separate lives. The middle son was named Craig. He and his wife, Shawna, were happy with their lives and decided to stay on the family compound with each other and their children. Son number four died in a hunting accident before a girl was kidnapped for him. The youngest son, Caleb, was married to Libby, and the couple had elected to stay on the compound and raise their family along with Craig and Shawna and their children."

"Wow. What a complicated case."

"It really was."

She'd finished her wine, so I offered her a refill, which she accepted. Georgia had made pear salads, so I decided that now was a good time to serve them. Once I brought the salads and the still warm from the oven bread out, I decided to ask about the case that had brought her here to Holiday Bay.

Thankfully, she launched right in. "Grover McClellan killed five couples beginning in two thousand fifteen. We know this for a fact. I wasn't part of the team who profiled and eventually caught up with him, but I think there is little doubt that this man is guilty of the deed he's doing a life sentence for. Then a month ago, you found the burial site here in Holiday Bay. From what seemed to have come from out of nowhere, McClellan asked to speak to his attorney and confessed to killing the eleven people you found buried in the mass grave. These eleven people had been killed in the late nineteen eighties, so we weren't sure he was telling the truth."

"Why the gap?" I asked. "Why would this man kill eleven individuals and bury them here in Maine in the late nineteen eighties, go dormant for so many years, and then kill ten people, which he was later prosecuted for?"

"According to McClellan, he originally had twelve victims picked out during his time on the East Coast in the eighties. Six men and six women, representing six couples. I guess couples were his thing since he was sent to prison three years ago for killing couples as well. Anyway, according to McClellan, victims number eleven and twelve were a young couple he'd met in a bar and intended to kill, but after he killed the man, he found he couldn't kill the woman. Long story short, McClellan claims to have fallen in love with victim number twelve, so he moved across the country with her, got a job, and apparently stopped killing. On the surface, based on what we've been told, it appears that McClellan and victim number twelve, whose name was Connie Fuller, had a happy life together. Then in two thousand fifteen, Connie died after a long battle with cancer, and McClellan started killing again."

"Five couples in less than three years."

"Exactly."

"So why would this man confess to killing the people in Maine if he didn't do it? Why would he confess to doing it if he did do it? That part makes no sense."

"McClellan wants to get married again," Sydney shared. "Apparently, he's been corresponding with a woman who thinks the story of a man so broken-hearted over the death of his wife that he goes on a killing spree choosing happy couples as his victims is a romantic one."

That comment made me wrinkle my nose. "Really?"

"Really."

I honestly didn't get people sometimes. "Okay, so even if this woman has fallen in love with McClellan, why would she want to marry him? I'm sure he must be in prison for life."

"He is, and trust me, there's no way he is ever going to be a free man. But there are women who are into that sort of thing. I suppose it's a safe relationship. This woman can be married yet assured that she's never going to have to share her toothbrush holder."

"Is this woman allowed to visit this serial killer?"

"She is as long as McClellan stays out of trouble. The visits are monitored, and McClellan is in chains the entire time. Not really all that romantic in my book, but I guess to each his own."

"Okay, so McClellan hopes to trade information about the eleven skeletons found in the burial site on a parcel of land I own for permission to get hitched?"

"Basically."

I leaned forward on my elbows. "Do you think McClellan did it? Do you think he killed the eleven people in the grave?"

"I wasn't sure at first, but after talking to McClellan and then speaking to the forensic team who are trying to identify the victims, I'm going to have to say yes, I do think he did it. McClellan knew details only the person who put those bodies in that grave could know. And given the fact there were six men and only five women, I'm inclined to believe the story of how he met his wife. McClellan says he can give us names for all the victims. If he can, that will close a lot of cases, and it will give eleven families closure. I'm inclined to give him what he wants in exchange for the information he claims to have, but that part isn't up to me. My job was simply to determine whether or not he's telling the truth."

"Which you seem to have done."

"Which I seem to have done," she confirmed.

Talk about a disturbing job. I guessed someone had to do it, but the whole thing left me feeling quite disturbed, so I decided it was time to change the subject to something a bit more pleasant. "I have sea scallops, saffron rice, asparagus, and baby carrots warming in the oven, although I can have Georgia make us something else if scallops don't work for you."

"I love scallops," she assured me.

"Okay. Go ahead and relax, and I'll grab the food. We can eat while we enjoy what's left of the evening."

Georgia had already made up the plates, so I just needed to slice a few more pieces of bread and bring the food to the deck. It really was a lovely evening, and so far, both the temperature and the bugs, or lack of bugs, had been cooperating.

"So tell me about your family," I said after the food had been served. "You mentioned that they live on Shipwreck Island."

"Yes." Her face lit up with the new subject. "My sisters and I grew up on the island after our parents died, and we went to live with our aunt. Aunt Charley runs a resort on the south end of the island, which her father-in-law, Hank, owns. Hank retired at one point, but after Charley's husband, Uncle Bobby, died, he moved back to the resort to help out."

"Sounds like a functional family dynamic."

She chuckled. "I'm not sure I'd use the word functional, but it does work. After Bobby passed away and Hank decided to move back to the resort to help Charley run things, I thought the pair would kill each other since both Hank and Charley are strong-willed and opinionated individuals. And while there is some fussing and grumbling between the two from time to time, they generally get along and really seem to work well together. And not only has Hank proven to be a good business partner for Charley, but he's really good with Emily's girls."

"Emily's girls?"

"Emily is the middle sister," she explained. "She left the island when she married, but when her husband was killed in an auto accident a year ago, Emily moved back to the island with her two daughters. The three of them currently live at the resort with Charley, Hank, and my youngest sister, Rory."

"I'm sorry to hear about your brother-in-law. I know firsthand how hard it is to lose a husband."

Sydney's face softened. "It really was hard for Emily and the girls at first, and I know we all wish we could rewind time and hope for a different outcome, but I think my sister and nieces are learning to deal with their new reality. Emily seems happy helping out at the resort, and the girls bounced back rather quickly once they understood that they were safe and didn't need to be afraid of all the changes. I think it helps that there's so much family to lean on. As I mentioned, my youngest sister, Rory, lives with my aunt as well. She works as a veterinary technician, and she frequently brings home animals in need of fostering. The girls love to pitch in and help."

"It sounds like you have a great family. There's been tragedy in the past, but you all seem so close. Like you're really there for each other."

"Oh we are." Her blue eyes flashed with conviction. "No matter what, family comes first."

Being part of a large blended family sounded wonderful. In a way, a blended family was what Georgia, Jeremy, Annabelle, and I had created. "I've never visited the island but have always wanted to. It sounds like a lovely place. Do you get to visit often?" I asked as I sliced a scallop in half and took a bite.

She frowned. "More often now that I've relocated to the West Coast, but not as often as I'd like. I'm afraid my job is a demanding one. The hours are sporadic, and any plans that might have been arranged take second place to a new case or a break in an existing case."

"It sounds like that might make it hard to develop relationships outside of work."

"It is," she admitted.

I was about to ask about the case she'd been called back to deal with when my cell phone rang. It was Colt. "I'm sorry, but I really need to get this."

"No problem. Go right ahead."

"Hey, Colt," I greeted after heading inside the cottage.

"I'm sorry I didn't call earlier, but it's been a crazy day."

"I heard about Henry Goodman. Two murder victims in two days are more than enough to make anyone crazy. Any leads?"

"Not really. It does appear that the same person killed both men. There's a lot to process, but I think I've done what I can do for today. I thought I might come over if you aren't busy."

"Sure, although you should know that Sydney Whitmore is here."

"Your dinner. I'm sorry I forgot all about that. I guess I'll just see you in the morning."

"No. I want you to come over. We're actually done eating, and I suppose I can make an excuse to send Sydney on her way once we have dessert, but I can't help but wonder if she might be able to help. This is a unique sort of case, and she is an FBI profiler."

He hesitated.

"It can't hurt to see if she wants to help."

"Yeah," Colt said, sounding tired. "I guess it couldn't hurt to ask. I'll be there in about an hour. I don't suppose you have leftovers I can scrounge?"

"I'm sure Georgia has something. Just get here when you can. I'll have something ready for you to eat."

After I hung up, I called Georgia to see what she might have for Colt to eat and then returned to the deck where Sydney was waiting. "I'm sorry about that. That was my friend, Police Chief Colt Wilder, on the line." I paused. "Actually, we're more than friends. We're dating." I wasn't sure why I felt the need to explain that, but it somehow seemed important. "He called to let me know he hadn't returned my previous calls since he's been swamped with two murders in two days."

"Wow. Two murders is a lot for this little town."

I nodded. "They seem to be related." I took a minute to describe everything I knew about the two deaths. "I don't suppose you have an idea as to what the killer might be trying to tell us?"

"I'd need to know more to offer an opinion. These things usually turn out to be more complex than they appear on the surface."

"Yeah. I have a feeling that might turn out to be the case, although both men were involved in local politics to a degree, so that seems to be the link that stands out at this point."

I shared the background of each of the two victims as well as the theories I'd entertained to date. She asked a few questions but didn't offer much in terms of a theory of her own. I offered Sydney dessert, but she indicated that she was stuffed and couldn't eat another bite. We continued to chat about topics of a general nature, such as favorite restaurants in San Francisco and people we thought we both might know, given the fact that she worked in law enforcement, as had my husband. Once Colt arrived, Sydney got up to leave. I suggested she stay, and when Colt agreed with my suggestion, she sat back down and listened to what he had to say.

Chapter 6

After Colt arrived, I went to the inn to get his dinner while he chatted with Sydney, and the two got to know each other. He'd brought photos of the two victims as well as the plastic clams each had held between their hands.

"As you can see, the victims were posed just the same," Colt said as Sydney looked at the photos. "Both men were lying on their right side with their legs bent at a ninety-degree angle at the hip. The legs were then bent again at the knee, with their arms laid one over the other, making it appear as if the men were asleep."

"Or praying," Sydney said.

Colt glanced at the photos again, "Yes. I suppose if they were upright rather than laying down, they would look as if they were praying."

Sydney picked up a photo of one of the plastic clams. "And each man had one of these between their layered hands?"

He nodded. "This week is Clam Bake week in Holiday Bay, and these clams are all over town. I know the theater company Abby hired to put on the murder mystery this Saturday is planning to use them to distribute clues, and there are a couple of booths at the kiddie carnival in town that will be using these same clams as well."

"It's too bad they're so widely available. If they weren't, they'd provide a clue in and of themselves. What about whatever was inside the clams? I assume they contained something."

Colt nodded. "Each had a note with a single word. The note in the clam of the first victim, Oliver Halifax, said greed, and the note in the hand of the second victim, Henry Goodman, said pride."

Sydney looked at the photos again. She didn't say anything for a minute, but I could tell she was processing what she saw. "What can you tell me about each of these men?"

Colt took a moment and then answered. "Oliver Halifax was a forty-one-year-old Holiday Bay resident. He was a successful investor who worked from home. He recently ran for and was elected to the town council, and it has been rumored that he cheated in order to stack things in his favor. A lot of the folks who've heard about Oliver's death assume it was the election and his involvement with the council that led to his death."

"Was the man married?"

Colt nodded. "Married but no children."

She set Oliver's photo aside. "Tell me about Henry Goodman."

"Henry was a thirty-eight-year-old real estate agent. Like Halifax, he was a bit of a workaholic and had done well for himself. He was single and didn't have any children."

"Cause of death?"

"Both men were injected with a serum that consisted of a barbiturate, paralytic, and potassium. They were killed somewhere other than where they were found. Both men were left in locations associated with Clam Bake week festivities if that helps. Halifax was found on the island where the murder mystery and clam bake is to take place, and Goodman was found in the gazebo in the park where the bands were going to play."

I jumped in. "I think it might be important to know that Georgia was called by someone she hadn't previously spoken to who sent her to the island to get photos, and Buck was sent to the gazebo by someone claiming there was an electrical problem."

"Do you know who called?"

I answered. "A man named Matthew Layton called Georgia about the photos. He said he was with the theater company putting on the murder mystery."

"And the name of the person who called Buck?" Sydney asked.

"Buck said that the man identified himself as one of the band members who was supposed to play that night. He said he stopped by to check out the sound system and found the electrical panel messed up. Buck didn't ask for additional information from the man. He just said he'd check it out," Colt answered.

"And was there a problem with the electrical?" Sydney asked.

"No," Colt confirmed. "The call was an obvious ploy to get Buck over to the gazebo."

Sydney sat back in her chair. "So the killer wanted the bodies to be found, and he or she wanted them to be found by a specific person at a specific time and not simply by whoever wandered by first. If they hadn't cared about who found the bodies or when they were found, they wouldn't have bothered to make the calls." Sydney looked at Colt. "Did you trace the phone numbers used to call both Georgia and Buck?"

He nodded. "Both calls were made from unregistered cells. The calls were made from different numbers, although I have to agree with you that one person likely made both calls."

"Using a burner for a single purpose and then dumping it is common in these situations. Tracing the call back to the owner seldom works, but I might be able to get information as to where the call was made if you're interested."

"I'm interested," Colt said. "Do you think we are looking at a serial killer?"

Sydney paused. "Perhaps, but at this point with only two victims. It's highly likely that you have a killer with a personal grievance with both men. If additional victims show up, then you might consider a serial killer, but for now, I'd look for a link between the victims."

"So you'd look for people with motive to want both men dead," I said.

She nodded. "Yes. At this point, I'd look for a personal motive, although the terms greed and pride can have religious and metaphysical meanings as well."

"Anything else?" I asked.

"The use of lethal injection as a murder weapon seems relevant. It's quick and fairly non-violent compared to other forms of murder. It might indicate that the killer knew his victims and wasn't necessarily looking to torture the men but simply kill them for some perceived wrongdoing. The killer may even consider himself to be the good guy, a vigilante of sorts who is ridding the world of wrongdoers." She looked at Colt. "I didn't ask about bank records or phone logs. I assume you didn't find anything relevant that might provide a different perspective."

He shook his head. "The bank records of both men appear to follow a regular sort of pattern for each individual. I didn't find any red flags amongst the phone records, although a lack of records during certain windows seems to indicate that both men had an unregistered cell phone that they used at times."

"And what about the movement of each of the victims before their deaths?"

"Oliver Halifax was last seen leaving his home just before noon on the day he died. His maid stated that he hadn't said where he was going but that it wasn't uncommon for him to come and go during the day, so she didn't think a thing about it. According to the calendar on his cell phone, he was supposed to meet with a man named Timothy Viscount, but I spoke to Mr. Viscount, and he said that Halifax called earlier that morning to cancel their appointment."

"Was his car found?" I asked, realizing that he'd been found on an island, so his car had probably been abandoned.

"It was found in the parking lot at the marina," Colt answered. "No one I spoke to remembered seeing Oliver there that day, although he did own a boat that he kept there. The boat was found in its usual slot, but it might have been taken out earlier, or Halifax could have gone to the marina to meet someone at the boat but was detained before they ever left the marina."

"And Henry Goodman?" Sydney asked.

"Mr. Goodman lives alone and never showed up at his office today. It's impossible to know exactly when he might have fallen prey to his killer. He keeps his own calendar rather than depending on a secretary, which we've yet to find. His computer is locked, and his cell phone is missing. I checked with his office, and no one has called to report that he missed an appointment he had with them, so at this point, I'm figuring he either canceled or didn't have any appointments today."

Colt's cell phone rang, and he got up to answer it. After he returned, Colt, Sydney, and I discussed the situation a while longer, and then Sydney excused herself to return to her suite.

"So what did you think of what she had to say?" I asked Colt after Sydney left.

"She didn't have a lot to add, but she did make a few good points. I'm sure that with more deaths to provide additional raw data, she'd be able to come up with a more complete profile."

"I hate the fact that murder victims are looked at as raw data."

Colt put his arm around me and pulled me in closer. "Me too. I'm sure those who deal with mass murders have to look at the victims as nothing more than raw data, or it would drive them crazy."

I supposed Colt had a point.

"It's a nice night. Do you want to take a walk?" I asked.

"I'd like a walk. A short one. I'm pretty tired, and I'll need to get up early."

Colt and I grabbed the dogs and then walked along the bluff. Colt's presence along with the warm glow of the stars and the sounds of the sea worked to calm my soul. The peace and calm of the moment allowed me to pretend that life was perfect, and concepts such as serial killers and mass killings weren't topics common enough to bother discussing. In the cold light of day, where rational thought took over from moonlight fantasy, it was frightening to even consider the possibility that our little town might actually be home to someone intent on killing multiple people for a reason only the killer himself would really understand. I didn't understand how Sydney did what she did or why she would choose to live in a reality where serial and mass killings were generally the topic of the day. But I supposed we should be grateful for people like her because, without those willing to step into the mind of a killer, the world, in general, would be helpless to stop them.

Chapter 7

Colt left early the following morning, so I got up early as well and dressed for the day. I figured I'd head over to the inn and visit with any of the guests who'd come down for breakfast, and then once everyone had dispersed, I'd check in with Sydney and see what her plans were for the day. I knew she had a flight out today, but I couldn't remember if she'd mentioned what time that flight was scheduled for.

"Morning," I said to Samantha, who was sitting alone at a table on the patio, sipping a cup of coffee.

"Morning," she replied, bending over to pet Rufus who'd walked up to say hi. "It's a gorgeous morning."

"It is," I agreed, glancing at the journal she appeared to have been writing in before I came over. "I didn't mean to interrupt your quiet time."

She held out a hand. "It's fine. Really. Have a seat."

I pulled out a chair and sat down. The sounds of the waves crashing and seagulls squawking in the distance brought me a sense of contentment that was hard to duplicate. Add a dash of sea air and the slight hum of bees in the garden, and you had a near-perfect recipe for a lazy summer morning.

Samantha continued her thought. "I didn't realize who you were when I first arrived, but one of the others told me that you're actually mild-mannered Abby Sullivan by day and bestselling author Abagail Sullivan by night."

I laughed. "Well, I don't know about all of that, but yes, I am Abagail Sullivan, the writer. Although, to be honest, I do most of my writing during the day."

She smiled. "Fair enough. I remember reading that Abagail Sullivan was based in San Francisco. What made you decide to move clear across the country to open an inn in Maine?"

I hesitated and then answered. "My son and husband were killed in an auto accident three and a half years ago. I guess I just needed a change after their deaths, so I moved here and opened the inn."

Samantha's smile faded. "Did it help? Moving and starting over?"

I nodded slowly. "Yes. I think it did." I paused and then continued. "I understand that you're dealing with your own loss. I'm not an expert on grief by any means, but if you want to talk about it..." I let the sentence dangle.

She didn't speak at first. Her gaze grew distant, and for a moment, I considered getting up and leaving her with her thoughts. But she eventually began speaking.

"Billy and I met when we were in the tenth grade." She smiled a sad little half-smile. "We dated all through high school, and when we graduated, we started a country-western band. We weren't anyone back then, and most of our gigs were free concerts in local bars, but eventually, we were noticed, and our little sideline actually began to make money."

I sat quietly and let her set the pace. The way she was staring into space was almost as if she wasn't even aware of my presence.

"Billy and I were happy. We had this tiny studio apartment, and we both worked crap jobs to afford our basic expenses. But in the evenings, we had our music and each other." She took in a deep breath and blew it out slowly. "I really thought we had a future, but then I was offered the chance to go on the road with the Harvey Tucker Band."

I knew that Harvey Tucker's country-western band had been popular back in the nineties.

"I really wanted to go, but Harvey Tucker only wanted me as a single and not the band. Billy and I talked it over, and somehow I convinced him that my jumping on this opportunity was the best thing for all of us, so I went on tour, promising to be back when it was over."

"But you never did go back," I took a guess.

She shook her head. "I never did. Once the tour was over, I moved to Nashville, and my career took off. I stayed in touch with Billy for a while, but when he refused to move to Nashville with me, I knew that what we'd had was over. I can't say that we ever officially broke up. It was more that we let the relationship die. I missed the friendship we'd shared and the couple we'd become over time, but I was focused on the charts and my solo career and never really looked back."

"And then?" I asked, realizing there had to be an "and then" before the end of this story.

"And then, about ten years ago, I ran into Billy. We were both in New York and just happened to show up at the same restaurant. We were each on our own, so we decided to eat together. By the end of the meal, old feelings had been reignited, and I ended up at his hotel. At the end of our stay, we parted ways, but we promised to meet again at the same hotel at the same time the following year if we were both still single. We ended up meeting eight more times. Three weeks once a year was all we had, but somehow it was enough."

I felt my stomach muscles tense as I sensed what came next.

"Then this past spring, I showed up at the hotel at the same time that we always met, but he didn't show.

I thought he might have met someone and chose not to come, but I later found out that he'd passed away the previous winter." She wiped a tear from the corner of her eye. "I know the relationship we shared was unconventional, and if either of us really cared, we could have worked out a way to spend more than three weeks a year together, but what we had worked for us." She took in a breath. "Or at least I thought it did at the time. Now that he's gone, I realize I would give anything, including my career, for more time with the only man I'm ever going to love."

"I'm so sorry." I laid my hand over hers.

She quirked her lips to one side. "Most people seem to feel inclined to discount the depth of my mourning since I wasn't willing to commit to this man in life. They figure that my inability to settle down equates to a lack of caring. But I did care. I do care. I always will." She looked around the area. "I really needed some time with my thoughts. I'm glad I came here. This setting is so cathartic, and Emma and Joel have helped a lot as well."

"How was the national park yesterday?" I asked, deciding to change the subject to something less emotional.

"It was fabulous. Today, the three of us plan to take a drive north. I'm really looking forward to it. Joel knows so much about the history of the area." She smiled. "He likes to narrate as we drive, which is fine with me. I can see that it's fine with Emma as well." She paused and then continued. "As hard as this has been for me, I know it has been ten times as hard for Emma. I can't imagine how difficult it must be to move on with your life when you've been married to the same man for almost fifty years."

"When you lose a spouse, everything changes," I agreed. "After Ben died, I had a hard time making the simplest decisions. What to have for dinner. What to watch on TV. The two of us had a rhythm that was just gone."

"But it does get better. Right?"

I nodded. "It does. I don't think the grief of losing a loved one ever really goes away, but you eventually find a way to live in the world without the person you were so dependent on."

"I think my grief has more to do with regret than a disruption to my life flow. Other than for three weeks a year, Billy really wasn't part of the decisions I made that got me through each day."

Samantha looked up and waved. Joel and Emma were heading our way. When they arrived at the table, I greeted them both, and we chatted as a group for a few minutes before I made my excuses and headed toward the inn.

When Rufus and I entered the kitchen through the back door, we found it empty. Continuing into the dining room, I found Chris, Sydney, Jeremy, Georgia, and Annabelle sitting at the table eating crepes and talking. I poured myself a cup of coffee and joined them.

"So what are we talking about?" I asked.

"Chris was just telling us about his research in the area," Georgia explained.

"I guess I never asked what you were here to research," I said.

"It's sort of complicated, but basically, I'm looking at environmental factors on the migration, reproduction, and population of various sea mammals, particularly those on the protected species list. My study is general in nature at this point, and all I'm really doing is gathering data which I will then compare to data gathered in years past, but I'm hoping to use my findings to get funding for additional research."

"It would be so much fun to spend the whole day following whales and playing with dolphins," Annabelle said. "Maybe I'll be a marine biologist when I grow up."

"It can be interesting work," Chris agreed. "And fun at times as well, but the hours are long, and at times, the work itself is somewhat boring. But if you're really interested in your subject, it can be rewarding as well."

"Do you see sharks?" Annabelle asked.

He set down his fork. "Not on this trip, but I did a study south of Florida a few years ago, and the focus of the study had to do with the migration of shark populations and food supplies. It was a two-year study and really interesting."

"I'd be scared if I saw a shark," Annabelle said.

"It can be dangerous, so you have to be aware of your surroundings when you're in the water. The men and women on the team I worked with on the project had spent a lot of time researching sharks and generally understood shark behavior, so the chance of injury was minimal." He smiled. "Actually, the only sea creature to take a bite out of me in all my years doing what I do was a sea lion off the coast of California. Those buggers are cute, but they can be aggressive as well."

Annabelle frowned. "Sea lions bite?"

"This one did, but I wouldn't worry too much. Generally, sea lions will leave you alone."

"What's the biggest animal you ever swam with?" Annabelle asked.

"A blue whale off the coast of Newfoundland. The sucker was huge. Close to a hundred feet, although I wasn't in a position to take measurements. I almost jumped out of my wetsuit when it swam up next to me."

Annabelle continued to ask questions, and Chris continued to answer. It was an interesting discussion, but I really wanted to talk to Sydney again before she left for the airport, so I suggested a walk.

"It must be fun to have so many different guests, each with their own story to tell," she said as we set off down the bluff with the dogs.

"I have to admit that I've met some very interesting people since opening the inn. Several of our guests have decided to stay in the area, and I consider them to be friends, and others send notes and emails after returning to their homes. Georgia really tries to get to know each guest."

"Georgia reminds me a lot of my sister, Emily. Given its location and the amenities offered, the resort at Castaway Bay has always been a very cool place to visit, but when Emily moved home, she brought something more. She's the frosting on the cake that seems to give the resort its heart."

"Does she take the time to get to know the guests?"

Sydney nodded. "Not only that, but she has this very calming and nurturing side to her. Emily's not only a fantastic mother, but she's the domestic diva of the family as well. She loves to cook and sew, and she's always planning parties and events. Emily does crafts with the guests, which many declare is the reason they come back every year. And most importantly, she has a knack for remembering the little things about each guest, like their favorite flower or favorite meal. She just has that special something that makes a great place to vacation feel like coming home."

I smiled. "I get that. Georgia is the same way. I think the ability and desire to connect personally with everyone you meet is a trait you're born with. I'm interested in our guests, and I want them to have a pleasant stay, but it's Georgia who makes everyone who stays with us feel like family. I'd love to meet Emily someday."

"You should totally come and visit the resort. It's really something special. And bring Georgia if you can both manage to get away at the same time. I'm sure she would get along great with Emily. They really are very similar."

"I'll try to work it out to make the trip west, and I hope you'll let me know if you come back to Maine in the future."

"I will. I've really enjoyed my short stay. I wish I could have stayed longer, but duty calls."

"You mentioned that you've been called back early to deal with a different serial killer than the one you came here to investigate. Can you talk about that case?"

She hesitated. "I suppose I can tell you the parts that have already been reported by the press. None of that is a secret, and it's all information you can find on your own. Beyond that, I can't really share the details about an ongoing case."

"I get it. That's fair."

She slowed her pace a bit as she began to speak. "The serial killer I've been called back to deal with hasn't been identified yet. What we know is that someone killed a woman named Patricia Taylor in June of two thousand eleven. She was twenty-eight at the time and had worked as an insurance agent. Her body was found floating in the bay, and her killer was never identified. Then in March of two thousand twelve, the body of a cocktail waitress named Crista Allen was also found floating in the bay, as were Lois Starlight in December of two thousand thirteen, Jessica Hamilton in two thousand fourteen, and Michelle Post and Ellen Pomeroy in two thousand fifteen. Following that, Fran Martin was found in April of two thousand sixteen, Aileen Waters was found in October of that same year, and Rena Stewart was found the following December. In all, there were nine women found between June of two thousand eleven and December of two thousand sixteen."

"I remember that," I said. I'd been living in San Francisco at the time. The women's deaths had been all over the news once it was suggested that a single person had carried out all the deaths. "Each of the victims had a new tattoo on their shoulder when their body was found. A Roman numeral number two."

Sydney nodded. "Yes. Each victim did have a new tattoo which law enforcement believe was part of whatever process this killer adhered to. You probably also remember that the killings stopped after Rena's body was found in December of two thousand sixteen. At least for a while. Then, in March of last year, a woman named Josie Stanton was found floating in the bay with the same tattoo."

"Might you have a copycat on your hands?"

"We considered that, but there were other details I can't comment about that led us to believe that Josie was killed by the same person who went on a spree beginning in two thousand eleven."

"And have there been others?" I asked.

She nodded. "After Josie, Tracy Longinese was found floating in the bay in November of last year, and Susana Parks was found in April of this year. The body of a nurse's aide was discovered this past Tuesday. The remains fit the same MO as the other women."

"Which is why you were called home."

She nodded.

"I know you probably can't say much beyond what you've already told me, but do you have any idea who might be doing this?"

She frowned. "Who? No. But after Josie turned up dead, I went back through the notes of everyone who'd worked on the case, and I found something no one had noticed before. Actually, I found a couple somethings, and while I can't comment on what I found, I can say that I think we have a much better profile now."

I couldn't help but notice the fire in her eyes. The passion. I certainly wouldn't get so worked up if all I had to look forward to were long days and even longer nights trying to think like a killer, but Sydney looked as if she was both ready and confident.

"Well, I hope you catch up with this guy before he kills again. It seems odd that there was such a long break between the victim in October two thousand sixteen and the one in March of last year, but maybe he was in jail for something else or perhaps, like McClellan, he met a woman and decided to stop."

"Maybe. I guess we can ask the guy about the gap once we catch him."

I was about to respond when my cell phone rang. "It's Colt. I should get this."

"Go right ahead."

"Hey, Colt," I said and then listened.

"There's been another murder."

"Who?" I asked as the knot in my stomach tightened.

"Stan Fairfield."

I knew that Stan was a dentist in town. I guess he must be around forty. Married. No children that I knew of.

"What happened?"

"I received an anonymous call this morning alerting me to the fact that the shed on the lot near Christmas Avenue where the kiddie carnival is held each year was in the process of being burglarized. When I arrived, I found the door to the shed open. When I went inside, I found Stan on the floor. He was posed in the same position as the others. He also had a clam between his hands, and the note in his clam said lust."

I glanced at Sydney. "It happened again. There's been another murder." I returned my attention to Colt. "Is there anything I can do?"

"I was actually hoping Sydney was still at the inn. Now that we have three victims, I wondered if she could take another look. I'm really worried about this. Three deaths in three days is a lot. It feels like a spree, and I'm afraid that it might not be over."

"Hang on." I looked at Sydney. "Colt wonders if you might have time to stop by his office and look at the photos of all three victims. Three murders in three days is a lot for our little town."

"I have time if we head into town now."

I told Colt that we were out walking but would return to the inn so Sydney could pack, and then we'd both be by in an hour or so. The idea that Holiday Bay might have its own serial killer terrified me more than I could say.

Chapter 8

Sydney followed me into town. She would need to leave directly from Colt's office if she was going to make her plane, but luckily, she'd booked a flight for late in the day rather than early in the morning, as I probably would have done.

"Thanks for taking the time to stop by," Colt said after ushering the two of us into the conference room where he had photos splayed out across the table. "I assume Abby filled you in on the fact that we have a third victim."

She nodded. "Three victims in three days does feel like a spree. And I agree, there could very well be others if we can't figure out who's doing this." She picked up a photo. "You said that the first man was an investor who worked from home, the second victim was a real estate agent, and the third a dentist."

Colt nodded. "That's correct."

"I seem to remember you also said that victims one and two had similar personalities. Both were Type 'A' workaholics who were financially successful but didn't seem to have extensive interpersonal relationships. Halifax was married with no children, and Goodman was single with no children if I remember correctly."

Colt nodded. "Right again."

"How about the newest victim, Stan Fairfield? Was he married?"

"Married with no children same as Halifax," Colt answered.

"All the men were in their late thirties to early forties. All were white with dark hair and a medium build. I'm not sure that looks and ethnicity play a role in this one, but it is good information to have." Sydney picked up a stack of photos and thumbed through them. "I'm wondering about the timing of the spree. All three men have lived in Holiday Bay for a while. As far as you know, have there been any other murder victims fitting this basic profile? Any murders that have gone unsolved to this point?"

"No," Colt answered. "I checked back ten years, but nothing popped. At least nothing locally."

She paused and studied one of the photos. "Abby said you received a call early this morning alerting you that a shed housing carnival props was in the process of being burglarized, but when you showed up to check it out you found the body of Stan Fairfield instead."

Colt nodded. "That's correct."

"I assume you didn't recognize the voice of the person on the other end of the line."

"No. It was a male voice. Deep. So deep it sounded intentionally altered."

"Any noise in the background?"

"Nothing that stood out."

Sydney flipped through a few more photos. "The man who called. How did he reach you? 911? Central dispatch? Landline for the local office?"

Colt frowned. "My cell, actually."

"Do a lot of folks you don't know personally have your cell phone number?" she asked.

"Yes and no. The Holiday Bay office is small. It's just me and one or two rookies doing their time before they can get a transfer to another office. I have a receptionist, Peach, but she only works a nine to five sort of schedule. If I've spoken to someone and need him or her to call me back, I'll ask them to call my cell, so it is out there. I guess enough folks know the number that if someone who didn't have it wanted to call me, they could find someone to give it to them."

She raised a brow. "I assume you checked the number the call originated from."

"I did. It's an unregistered cell phone that appears to be turned off. Same as the others."

"Georgia was also called, as was the owner of the hardware store. I think I remember his name was Buck. Do we know how they received their calls?" she asked.

"The call to Georgia went to her cell, which didn't stand out as odd because the person she spoke to told her he was from the theater company that had been hired to put on the murder mystery tomorrow night. The call to Buck went directly to the landline at his hardware store," Colt answered.

Sydney set the stack of photos she'd been looking at down and picked up another stack. "It sounds as if this person is either a local or, if not a local, a visitor who has been around long enough to know that Georgia had hired the theater company and that your cell phone number was accessible. At this point, my money is on the killer being a resident. Assuming this is true, I have to wonder why now. Why did this person who has probably been living in the same town as his victims for some amount of time start killing now? And why link the deaths to the clam bake via the plastic clam each victim held?"

"I suppose something about the clam bake could be the trigger," I offered. "Like maybe something happened to this person at last year's clam bake that was never resolved emotionally. Maybe as the weeklong event neared, it triggered whatever rage he'd been holding inside to that point, and he snapped."

Sydney smiled at me. "That's actually a good theory to a point. The murders are neat. They are precise and organized." She looked down at the photos. "The men were injected with a mixture that will kill them almost immediately. Once they are dead, all the bodies are moved to a location that I believe must have importance of some sort. Once the bodies are posed and the clues left, the killer calls someone to make sure the bodies are found, and he seems to care who finds them and when. I haven't had the chance to inspect the bodies, but it appears that none of the men were beaten or tortured." She looked at Colt. "I'm assuming there was no sign of sexual assault."

"That's correct. There's no sign that the men had been held for any length of time before being killed. The medical examiner didn't find any ligature marks to indicate that either their hands or ankles had been tied. Additionally, as you just indicated, there is zero evidence that the men were beaten or abused in any way. My feeling is that the killer knew these men and this allowed him to be in close proximity to them. He injected them with the serum, causing them to fall to the ground and eventually die. Then he moved and posed them. Shortly after the men were posed, he made the call to whoever he wanted to find the body."

"So what's the deal with the clams?" I asked.

"When considered as a set, pride, greed, and lust generally indicate that the killer is fixated on morality. Those specific terms bring to mind the seven deadly sins. It's a commonly used theme which, in my opinion, has been overused, but I can see the appeal."

"Seven deadly sins? So does that mean that there will be four more murders?" Colt asked.

Sydney nodded. "If my assumption at this point is correct, then yes, it is likely there will be four more murders."

"Like hell," he spat. "There's no way I'm going to let this guy kill four more people."

"I agree that it needs to stop now." She paused and then continued. "You said that clam bake was a weeklong event. Weeklong as in seven days?"

"Five, actually," Colt said. "The first day of events was yesterday, Wednesday, and the events run through Sunday."

"If the clam bake is the instigating event, as I suspect, then it's likely the other four murders will occur at some point between now and Sunday afternoon. That gives us almost no time to figure this out." She glanced toward the photos on the table. "I know a woman, Genevieve. She works for Ezra and is just about the best darn hacker on the planet. If you need information of any sort, she can get it. I can call her if you want. She might be willing to help narrow things down a bit."

"I would welcome her help if she's willing," Colt said.

"Okay." Sydney took her cell phone from her purse. "Give me a few minutes." With that, she left the room.

"So what do you think is going on?" I asked Colt after Sydney had left the office.

His lips tightened. "I'm not sure. When the only victim was Oliver Halifax, I thought there was some validity to the idea that his death might be due to his involvement with the town council and the debate over the proposed resort. When Henry Goodman died, I considered other options, but since Henry was involved in politics and the resort project, I still figured we'd find our killer by traveling down that particular highway. But Stan Fairfield is a dentist. I'm not sure how he fits the profile if the resort and the upcoming vote is at the heart of things."

"He might be an investor," I suggested.

Colt bobbed his head. "Perhaps. That's something I can look into. But if the resort and the upcoming vote are the motives, then why the clams? I feel like the killer is trying to send us down the metaphysical road in terms of motive."

"Perhaps that's intentional. Perhaps the clams and the clues contained within are being used as decoys, so you'll become sidetracked and don't focus on the real motive."

"You make a good point," Colt said. "While it might not be wise to discount the clues as key, I agree it would be a mistake to abandon other theories at this point."

Colt picked up one of the photos and appeared to be studying it. I was sure this was difficult for him. There had been murders in Holiday Bay in the past, but nothing like this.

"When I went by the Halifax home to notify his wife of his passing, she wasn't home. I did some checking, and it turns out that she's on a transatlantic cruise. I left a message with the cruise line for her and one on her cell, but she hasn't called back."

I waited for Colt to complete his thought since I could sense he wasn't finished.

"Stan Fairfield's wife is also out of town. I'm actually not sure where she is. One of their neighbors told me that she took off on a road trip to visit friends and wouldn't be back for at least a month. I've left messages for her as well, but so far, there's been no reply. Henry wasn't married, so there's no wife to notify. His closest relative is a cousin, and I've left a message for him to call me. I expect to hear back today."

"Do you think the fact that all three victims were currently living alone in their homes is relevant?" I asked.

"Maybe. As far as I can tell, none of the men were killed in their home, but I suppose they could have been abducted from there. The county guys went to all three homes looking for clues but didn't find anything. Still, it does seem like a huge coincidence that all three victims would have most likely been home alone in the house if they had indeed been abducted from there."

I was about to comment when Sydney came back in from making her call. "I spoke to Genevieve, and she's going to take a look at the information I sent and get back to me. I gave her basic information about each of the men, but the more we have to give her to feed into her software, the more likely we are to come up with something relevant. I think one of the things we need to do at this point is to come up with additional data on all the men."

"I'll organize what I have," Colt said.

"What does the press know at this point?" Sydney asked. "I assume the news of the death of at least the first man is out by now."

Colt nodded. "The local newspaper is published on Mondays and Fridays and distributed via local businesses. Additionally, there's an abbreviated online edition posted every day. Oliver Halifax's remains were found during the late afternoon Tuesday, so yesterday's online edition of the newspaper has a brief story simply letting folks know that he'd been found dead on the island, and while the cause of death hadn't been released, it looked like he hadn't died of natural causes."

"Does the press know about the clams and the notes?" Sydney asked.

"No," Colt answered. "We've kept that out of the press. I expect that today's online edition will have news of the second death as well as a bit more detail about the first death. It usually posts mid-morning. I haven't seen it yet."

"Let's take a look," Sydney suggested.

As Colt suspected it would be, the article today was a lot longer than the one the previous day. The man who wrote the paper had been out and about yesterday talking to folks and gathering quotes and opinions. While he was out researching the first victim, which had the local rumor mill operating at warp speed, news of the second victim had broken.

As Colt also predicted, the article didn't mention the clam or note. The author of the article didn't go into a lot of depth regarding the positioning of the body or the fact that the discovery of the victim had been facilitated by the delivery of a phone call.

Sydney pursed her lips and appeared to be thinking things over. Eventually, she spoke. "As long as the press and the public as a whole are kept in the dark about the specific details such as the clam and the note, we may be able to use that to flush this guy out. The killer obviously isn't trying to hide the fact that these men have been murdered. He obviously wants everyone to know they are dead, and it seems that he's interested in generating a good amount of gossip by the content of the notes he left behind. We have several options to consider. We could continue to keep things quiet. There are both advantages and disadvantages in doing so. We could hold a press conference and lay everything out on the table. There is a strategy to doing things this way as it helps maintain control of the narrative. We could also leak a lie or inaccuracy. If the killer is invested in sending a specific message, which seems to be the case, leaking a piece of information that contradicts what it appears he's trying to do might flush him out."

"What exactly do you think he's trying to do?" I asked.

"It depends," she said. "If the motive behind the deaths is to call out and punish these men, then the reason the notes were left behind might be to discredit these men even in death. If this is the case, then killing these men isn't enough. He wants the world to know the sort of person they really were. He wants to provide a spark to get people talking in the hope that the truth will come out and the sins of these men will be revealed."

"So leaking news that would shed light on good things the men had done, whether they had actually done these good deeds or not, might egg the killer into getting involved and saying something to set the record straight," I said.

"Perhaps. It does appear as if the killer is very methodical about each and everything he does. If nothing else, putting out a false statement might throw him off his game and cause him to make a mistake."

That made sense to me.

"What about floating the rumor that someone confessed to one of the murders and saying we didn't consider the deaths to be linked?" Colt asked.

"That could work," she agreed. "Although, it might be best to use the press to warn other men who might be potential targets, and the best way to do that is to disseminate accurate information. There are many strategies when it comes to using the press to gain a specific outcome, and each strategy contains its own set of pros and cons."

"Given the fact that there may be four more men on this killer's list, I'm not comfortable with disseminating anything less than the truth," Colt said. "I understand how the other strategy might work, but

I'm a lot more concerned with these four men than I am with anything else, including the arrest of the killer. Don't get me wrong, I want to catch this guy, but at this point, my primary goal is to stop the killing. It seems that the best way to do that is to lay it all out so the public can take steps to protect themselves."

"I don't disagree with that," Sydney said. "Especially given the impossibly tight timeline." She looked down at her cell phone. "It's Genevieve. Maybe she has something."

Sydney answered and then listened. She took notes but didn't say much in response. Since we could only hear her side of the conversation and she wasn't saying anything, I really wasn't sure if this woman had come up with something or not.

"Okay, thanks, Gen. We're still discussing the situation, so I may call you back looking for additional data."

With that, she hung up. She looked at Colt. "According to Gen, she found three things all three men had in common, which in my mind, gives us three places the killer might have met the men. As you've already mentioned, two of the men appear to have been wrapped up in the proposed development. Oliver Halifax was heavily invested in the project. So much so that he ran for the town council to make sure that the proposed project passed. Henry Goodman was working with the developer to obtain the proper permits. He'd been promised the listings when the portion of the resort reserved for timeshares was made available. And Stan Fairfield is involved through his wife, who is the sister of the architect who designed the whole thing. All had personal and financial incentives to see the development approved, so if it turns out the resort was the motive for murder, then it seems that we're looking for someone who had a lot to lose if the development was allowed to move forward."

"What do the clams and the notes have to do with the development?" I asked.

"Probably nothing," Sydney said. "It's possible the notes were left as a diversion meant to distract us." She looked at Colt. "Genevieve is looking at the phone and financial records for the company behind the resort and the major stockholders. It is likely that the killer isn't associated with the resort, but it doesn't hurt to see if we can find anything that might point to the instigating event."

"So in this case, the instigating event wouldn't be the clam bake," Colt said.

"It's not likely. If the resort is the motive, then the clam bake, plastic clams, and notes left in the clams are all likely meant to be camouflage."

"And the other two places where the three men overlap?" I asked.

"Interestingly, church. Not only are all three men members of the same community church, but all three attended a men's retreat almost exactly one year ago. While the men's involvement with the proposed resort is a good motive, the link to the church and the men's group fits the rest much more closely. Unless, as we've suggested, the whole thing with the seven deadly sins turns out to be a smokescreen, I think we might find the killer here."

"Which church do the men belong to?" I asked.

She looked at her notes. "The community church on Palm Avenue."

"That's Noah's church," I said.

"Noah?" she asked.

"The minister," I answered. "He's a good friend. I'll talk to him. If he knows something, I think he'll tell me. I'm not sure he'd share personal information about his parishioners with someone he doesn't know."

"Okay." Sydney nodded. "That works for me."

"And the third link?" Colt asked.

"All three men have made large payments to a company called Evagrius Industries. According to the webpage for Evagrius Industries, the company specializes in personal development. They hold seminars and publish books, those sorts of things. The thing I found the most interesting is that Evagrius Ponticus was a well-known speaker, thinker, and writer in the fourth century. His name is often linked to the concept of the seven deadly sins, along with a lot of other ideas, although it doesn't appear that Evagrius Industries focuses on religious or metaphysical themes."

"What do they focus on?" I wondered.

"It appears the focus is on personal wealth and power and harnessing these energies with focused intentions accompanied by hard work and financial savvy. I need to look into it further, but it doesn't appear that there is a religious basis for what is taught. Still, it does seem to be quite the coincidence that all three men made payments to a company named for a fourth-century thinker often associated with the deadly sins."

"It seems like a huge coincidence," Colt agreed.

Sydney glanced at the clock on the wall ticking down the seconds. "I'm afraid I really need to go. I'll call you when I arrive on the West Coast. Maybe I'll have a flash of insight while on the plane."

"I appreciate that," Colt said.

"I'll walk you out," I said to Sydney as she turned toward the door.

"Okay." She glanced toward where Colt was standing one more time. "Until next time."

Once we were outside, Sydney paused, seeming to understand that I wanted to speak to her in private.

"How exactly does someone with a cold case to solve contact Ezra Reinhold?" I asked.

Sydney raised a brow. "Do you have a cold case in need of solving?"

"Not really." I paused. "Well, sort of." I paused again and then continued. "It's just that after Ben died, I found some stuff of his that I'd had no idea he'd even had in his possession while he was alive. Files. Notes. Airline tickets. That sort of thing. I'm not sure why he kept this stuff from me because we were the sort of couple to share everything. I knew he liked to poke around in cold cases and even helped him at times, so there was no reason for him to keep anything from me. But he did."

Sydney waited for me to finish. I had to admire her restraint. I would have probably been trying to hurry me along if our roles had been reversed.

"Some things happened after Ben's death that shed light on the fact that he had things in his life that he chose not to share," I said, basically repeating myself. "Big things. Things that a husband probably should have shared with his wife. In the end, everything that I looked into or had Colt look into on my behalf only served to prove that Ben really was a good guy, but I guess the revelation of this other life caused me to wonder. Then, about a year ago, I received an official letter from SFPD Internal Affairs, letting me know that some of Ben's cases had been reviewed and that the process was complete, with all questions about his conduct answered and cleared. Until that point, I had no idea IA was even reviewing Ben's cases. I was glad he'd been cleared, but that, coupled with the little inconsistencies I'd already found, made me wonder even more."

Sydney took my hand in hers. She looked me directly in the eye. "I won't claim to know Ben well, but we did work together on the case of the missing teen, and based on everything I observed about him, he appeared to be a genuinely nice guy who really cared about people. It wasn't his job to track down this teenager. He hadn't been assigned the case, and he wasn't being paid for the time he committed to finding his answers. He did it because he cared. He did it to find this girl if she was still alive, and if she'd been killed, as most suspected, he did it to bring closure to the family."

"So is it your opinion that Ben probably wasn't wrapped up in anything illegal or shady?"

She nodded. "Yes, that's my opinion. I'm good at reading people. It's what I do, and my ability to spot a lie is what makes me so good at my job. If Ben was the sort to have had an ulterior motive for doing what he did, I think I would have picked up on that."

"And you didn't?"

She shook her head. "No, I didn't." She took a breath. "You were married to Ben. You knew him better than anyone. What does your gut tell you about him? Not your mind and not your heart, but your gut."

"My gut tells me that Ben was a good guy who really cared about people and would never do anything to hurt anyone."

She raised a brow.

"I know I should trust that. Colt has counseled me many times to trust that. And I do. To a point. But then I find something, or I find out something about Ben that I had no idea was going on, and it makes me feel less certain."

She let go of my hand. "I get it. I really do. It would be my advice to you to let go of all the things that are causing you to question the motive of the man you loved and just accept that he loved you and would never have done anything to hurt you or anyone else. But if you stumble across something specific that you find you just can't let go of, call me, and I'll see what I can do."

"Frank Ribaldi."

She frowned. "What about Frank Ribaldi?"

"He worked with Ben. Shortly after I moved to Holiday Bay, he emailed me looking for a file he thought Ben might have had at home when he died. Ben's files were in storage in San Francisco, so I told him I didn't have anything. Since then, I've collected the files, and I have to say his name has come up a lot. He was being investigated by IA at the same time that Ben was. Frank was cleared of wrongdoing as well, but I have a gut feeling that there's a lot more going on than anyone knows at this point."

"Unlike Ben, who I feel certain was a good guy, I don't have the same warm fuzzy feeling about Frank. I guess you heard he was shot and killed."

I gasped. "No, I hadn't heard. When?"

"A few months ago. Frank was shot by one of the gang members he'd been accused of taking bribes from. It seemed that even though he was cleared by IA, the gang members who felt he'd double-crossed them weren't quite as forgiving."

"Wow. I had no idea. Colt persuaded me to set the whole Frank Ribaldi thing aside, and I did. I hadn't really given it another thought until you showed up and reminded me of things."

She gave me a hug. "I think your instinct about Frank being a dirty cop was right on, but it seems that he got what he probably had coming to him. I'm sorry that Ben's association with Frank caused you to doubt your husband, but if you want my opinion, any lies Ben might have told or secrets he might have kept were simply to protect the woman he loved."

I hugged Sydney. "Thank you. I can't tell you how badly I needed to hear that."

Sydney promised to check in with me about our possible serial killer once she got back to the West Coast and then headed toward her car. Once she left, Colt announced that he had a list of men and women to speak to who he felt were associated with all three murder victims, so I headed across town to talk to Noah.

Chapter 9

Luckily, Noah was in his office when I arrived.

"Abby, what a nice surprise," he greeted, offering me a seat. "What brings you by today?"

I explained about the three murder victims and the fact that they all attended his church.

"Stan Fairfield is dead?" He looked legitimately shocked. "I hadn't heard. What happened?"

"I don't have all the details, but apparently, he was killed in the same manner as the other men."

"So you're tracking down all the connections the three men might have shared."

I nodded. "Colt might be by at some point to speak to you personally, but he's swamped with this one, so I offered to help out. Is there anything you can tell me about the three men that might help us figure out who might have done this?"

Noah took a deep breath. He leaned forward and rested his arms on the desk in front of him. "None of the men attend church on a regular basis, but they did all show up every now and again." He paused thoughtfully before continuing. "The only link that comes to mind is a men's retreat a group from the church attended a while back."

"Is this the retreat that was held almost exactly a year ago?"

Noah paused, I assumed to think it over. "Yes. I think it was just about a year ago."

"Did the church sponsor the retreat?"

"No. Stan approached me about a company named Evagrius Industries. They were hosting a retreat about an hour north of here. Stan wanted to use the church to recruit participants, so while I didn't endorse the retreat or sponsor it in any way, I did allow Stan to hand out fliers. I remember Oliver and Henry as being two of the men who attended."

"Do you know anything more about the actual retreat?"

"Not really. When I was approached by Stan, he gave me some literature to look at. The retreat wasn't the sort of thing the church would sponsor, but it looked harmless enough, and I could see how many of the ideas they were touting might be useful in everyday life."

"Do you remember seeing anything about the seven deadly sins in that literature?"

Noah frowned. "No. Nothing like that. The retreat seemed to be focused on issues other than religion. There were talks about success in business and community matters. I think there may have been a few things about relationships and personal growth, but nothing I saw even touched on the sort of doctrine you'd find here at church."

"Were there other men who attended this retreat?"

"Sure. I think around a hundred men from various small towns in Maine attended. There was a van from this church full of men who drove up together."

"Do you remember who all attended from this church?"

"Not offhand, but I may have a list." Noah stood up and walked out into the outer office, where Christy usually sat. He opened the file cabinet and started sorting through the folders.

"Is Christy off today?" I noticed that her desk was clear of clutter.

He nodded. "Christy's off this whole week while her friend, Rodney, is in town."

I wanted to ask Noah how he felt about that, but it was none of my business, so I didn't.

"Here it is." He pulled out a sheet of paper. "I'll make a copy for you." Once he'd run it through the copy machine, he handed me the copy.

"Seven names," I said.

He frowned. "And three are dead. Do you think these men died because of their link to that retreat?"

"I don't know," I answered honestly. "I'll give these names to Colt. He'll probably call to follow up."

I took my cell phone out and called Colt, but he didn't pick up, so I left a message.

"I'm going to see if I can track these four men down. Do you happen to know where I can find them?"

Noah looked at the list. "Travis Kubel, Don Perry, Lance Rivers, and Kurt Steadman." He paused. "Travis works at the tire store over on Shop Street. He should be there now. Don owns an insurance agency. He's in and out, but he should be in as well. Lance works construction. I can call around and see where he might be working today." He frowned. "I'm not sure about Kurt. I heard he was fired from his last job. I'm not sure where he ended up."

"Thanks," I said. "I guess I'll start with Travis."

"I'm going with you." Noah dug his keys out of his pocket.

"Are you sure you want to get involved?"

"I'm sure. These men are my parishioners. If they're in some sort of trouble, I want to be there to warn them personally.

Noah offered to drive, so I let him. He headed to the tire store where Travis worked. Luckily, he was in. Unlike the three victims, Travis had a family.

Additionally, unlike the three victims, who were all considered affluent, he was a blue-collar sort of guy with limited financial resources.

"Pastor Noah. What are you doing here?" Travis asked after the two of us approached.

"Abby and I would like to speak to you a minute." He looked around. "Is there somewhere private we can chat?"

"I guess we can step outside. There's a bench in the back where we stack the discarded tires."

"That would be fine," Noah said.

Once we were settled, I jumped in. "I'm not sure if you've heard, but there have been three murders in town."

"Three? I heard about Oliver, and someone just told me about Henry a while ago. Who's the third?"

"Stan Fairfield."

"Stan? Who would want to kill Stan?" Travis asked.

"That's what we're trying to figure out," I answered. "At this point, we're looking at commonalities between the three men. There are several," I admitted. "But one of the things the three men had in common was Noah's church."

"And the men's retreat a group attended last year," Noah added.

He paled. "Do you think I'm in danger?"

"We think you might be in danger," I answered. "We don't know that you are, but it's a possibility. We're not certain if the church or the retreat is the link we're looking for between the victims either. What we do know is that you're on a list of seven men, three of whom have been murdered in the past three days, who attended the men's retreat. We wanted to warn you, and we wanted to see what you might remember about the retreat."

The poor guy looked as if he was going to pass out.

"All three men who have died seemed to have been alone at the time of their deaths. Now that you know about the possible danger, you can take precautions," I assured him. "You're in a public place here at work, and there are a lot of people around, so I think you're safe for now. You'll just need to be careful when you walk to your car at the end of your workday or if you're alone at home. It also appears that at least one of the three victims may have gone to meet someone who'd contacted him before his death. If someone calls you and wants to talk, even if it's someone you know, don't go."

"My wife and I have plans to take the kids to Virginia Beach to visit her sister. We were going to leave tomorrow, but I think I'm going to pack up the car, and we'll leave today."

"I think that's a good idea. Before you go, however, I need to ask you about the retreat."

He looked at the ground.

"Did something happen that might be considered a motive for murder?"

He didn't answer at first.

"It's okay," Noah said. "Just tell us what you know."

"It's pretty embarrassing."

"That's fine. Noah and I don't shock easily. If the killer is connected to the retreat, anything you tell us could help us track him down."

Travis cleared his throat. "Stan invited me to attend the retreat, and to be honest, I was sort of undecided from the beginning. But you know Stan. He was a persuasive guy, and he convinced me that I had a lot of responsibility in my everyday life and that some quiet time to myself would be helpful. Anyway, I eventually agreed to go."

"Do you know why he tried so hard to convince you to attend?" I asked.

"He said something about needing seven attendees. I guess there was some sort of special rate for groups of seven or more. Anyway, when we first arrived, things looked pretty normal. A desk was set up to handle check-ins, and everyone was assigned a room in one of the long dormitory-style buildings. We had an hour to settle in, and then everyone was supposed to meet in the conference room for a welcoming ceremony. I found Don in the crowd, so I headed in his direction. I asked about the others, and he told me that Lance had been juggling a huge job with a remodel on his own house and was exhausted.

We both agreed that Lance probably wouldn't be seen until the following morning. Eventually, Kurt joined Don and me. He said that Stan, Oliver, and Henry had gone over to the get-together in the other building. I asked what building he was referring to, and he answered that there was another huge conference center across the lawn area. I was curious, but not overly so at this point. The speeches were about to commence, so Don, Kurt, and I all took our seats."

"And then?" I asked, hoping to move things along.

"After the welcoming speeches, everyone was free to break up and mingle. An open bar and plenty of appetizers were provided. Don went to work on the appetizers, and Kurt headed to the bar. I was curious about the other building, so I decided to take a walk and check it out. When I arrived, I found a lot more going on than team building and male bonding."

"What exactly did you find?" Noah asked.

"A scene that looked like a bachelor party complete with booze, gambling, and women."

I noticed that Travis wouldn't even look at Noah, but he seemed okay maintaining eye contact with me.

"Were any of the men in your group participating in this party event?" I asked.

He nodded. "Stan, Oliver, and Henry were all there. I didn't see anyone else at this point, but I'm pretty sure Lance actually was sleeping, and Don and Kurt were still in the main conference center, eating and drinking."

"So what did you do at this point?" I asked.

"I went back to join Kurt and Don. By the time I got there, Kurt was already smashed. I wasn't really in the mood to deal with a drunken Kurt, so I went to my room."

"And then?" I asked.

"And then I read for a while and went to bed. By the following morning, Lance had emerged and joined Don and me for breakfast. Don told us that Oliver, Henry, Stan, and Kurt were all at the other conference building, and he doubted we'd see them again. Lance joined Don and me at the first group meeting and then headed back to his room. Don was with me until lunch, but then one of the other men mentioned the food was much better in the party building, so he left as well. I attended the three remaining sessions that day."

"Were there other men in attendance?" I asked.

"Sure. I would say there were a hundred men overall. In the beginning, most were with the main group; however, slowly but surely, we started losing people. By Sunday, there were hardly any of us left in the power building sessions."

"So all the men from your group ended up in the party building?" I verified.

"All but Lance. He really was there to sleep. He joined me for a session every now and then, but most of the week was spent in his room."

"Did you go over to the party building at all?" I asked.

"I poked my head in a few times. Oliver started gambling and couldn't stop. I seriously feared that he'd end up bankrupting himself by the end of the trip. I tried to distract him by suggesting other options, but he was hooked, and there was no way anyone was getting him out of there until he either won all his money back or lost what was left."

"And Stan?"

"It was all about sex for him. The guy seemed to have a different girl on his arm each day and in his bed each night. I think Stan had been to a similar retreat the company had thrown at another location. He was the one pushing us all to go with him, and he was the first one to head to the party building."

Noah spoke for the first time in a while. "I can't believe I let Stan hand out fliers to a middle-aged frat party."

"You couldn't know. And there were sessions offered like the sort advertised for those who wanted to attend. What hadn't been advertised were the recreational opportunities that would also be offered. And it did seem like there was something for everyone. Kurt got blind stinking drunk his first night there and never sobered up until it was time to go home. He got in touch with his violent side and spent most of his time either fighting with other drunks with anger issues or sleeping it off as his body prepared for the next round. Don was more into the food. There was a twenty-four-hour buffet with all the greasy, fatty sugar-coated food you could eat. I think Don must have gained fifty pounds that week."

"And Lance?"

"Lance never did join in. At least not that I saw. Like I said before, he was sleeping most of the time. I was the only one who even attempted to attend the regular sessions, but by Sunday afternoon, I'd settled into a funk."

"Funk?" I asked.

"I guess I was conflicted. I'm not the sort to do the whole party thing, but I have to admit that the other guys were having a lot of fun. Oh, I was tempted to give in and join them, but I guess deep down, I knew that would make me miserable as well. I found myself unhappy with the decision to stay the course and attend the planned seminars, and I also found myself unhappy with thoughts of giving in and having some fun. I'm glad that I didn't cheat on my wife or gamble my life savings away, but I have to say that after having attended that week, I'm having a harder time being happy with my life the way it is." He looked directly at me. "Do you think the guys who died were killed because they chose to party rather than attend the seminars?"

"I don't know," I answered honestly. "I'm not sure that week is even part of what's going on. We're just trying to cover all our bases."

"I get it, and I'm grateful for the heads up. I think I'm going to call my wife about the change in travel plans." Before he wandered back inside, he assured Noah and me that he wouldn't allow himself to be alone and promised that he wouldn't arrange to meet up with anyone other than his wife, even if the Pope himself called for a meeting. Noah and I felt we'd done what we could to warn the guy, who may or may not even be in any danger, so we said our goodbyes and headed toward Don Perry's insurance office.

"What do you think the men's retreat with the sinner's option is really all about?" Noah asked as we drove across town.

"I'm not sure. At first, I thought the idea of a men's retreat was simply a cover that men could feed to their wives and significant others so they would be able to have a wild guy's week without getting any flack for it. But it sounded like even the guys don't know the real deal until after they get there. Travis did say that Stan seemed to know what was going on from the beginning, and he is the one who recruited the other six, so maybe it's one of those types of deals where once you're initiated, in order to return, you have to bring six other men."

"Maybe, but why? What does Evagrius Industries get out of it? If they simply want to provide party week for men, why the ruse?"

That was a good question. "I suppose the folks from Evagrius Industries might be blackmailing these men. Assuming they target men who tend to attend church and generally live a somewhat conservative lifestyle and it isn't simply a fluke that Stan happened to do his recruitment at a church, maybe the plan is to get these men to an out of the way place for the week without their wives, girlfriends, bosses, pastors, or clients, and then provide every sort of temptation for them to cut loose. Maybe these weeks are taped, and

Evagrius Industries then uses the tapes to get money or cooperation or something from these men."

Noah took a moment before answering. "I suppose that makes sense. Stan was married. I'm sure he wouldn't have wanted his wife to know that the annual men's retreat he attended was really a way for him to enjoy hot and cold running women without her knowing about it."

"And Oliver worked in investments. He handled a lot of money, and it sounds like he had a gambling problem. I imagine he'd have done whatever it took to keep his little gambling problem to himself."

"And Don had a heart attack a while back. I bet his wife and doctor had him on a strict diet."

"So the men who attend are tested. Some, like Travis, if he's telling the truth, avoid temptation and are probably of no future use to whoever is behind Evagrius Industries. But men like Oliver, Stan, and Henry with a lot to lose might become targets for future use. I remember that Sydney said that all three of our murder victims made payments to Evagrius Industries. That means that there's a good chance this wasn't the first weeklong retreat for any of them. Stan seemed to be the one who put the group together, but it's likely the others may have helped in some way."

"I guess we should ask the men if they've been contacted by anyone from Evagrius Industries since the retreat."

"I can also see if Sydney's friend, Genevieve, can find out if Travis, Don, Lance, or Kurt have made payments to the company."

Noah pulled into the parking lot next to the office building where Don Perry had an office. We both got out and headed toward the door with large lettering stating that insurance was sold there.

"Noah, Abby. What are the two of you doing here?"

"We'd like to speak to you in private," Noah said.

A look of concern flashed across the man's face. "Sure. I'm holding down the fort while my receptionist is out, but we can talk in my office."

Between Noah and me, we got the man up to speed. We shared pretty much everything we knew, figuring it was best to get right to the questions with answers we didn't know.

"I can't believe Stan is dead. I'd heard about Oliver and Henry, of course, and to be honest, I figured their deaths were related to the political nightmare associated with that new development."

"And they may have been," I jumped in. "At this point, we don't know anything. And I think it is important to point out that we don't know whether or not you might be a potential target. We're looking at every angle and warning everyone we can think of to warn."

"And I appreciate that. I'm going to head home after we finish here and talk to my wife about spending the weekend at her mother's. She's been nagging me to go for weeks. She'll be thrilled."

"In the meantime, don't agree to meet anyone," I cautioned. "It appears that at least one of the victims was heading out to meet someone when they were last seen."

"I'll go straight home after speaking to you and be on the road to my mother-in-law's shortly after that." He looked at me. "What do you need from me?"

"Travis filled us in on the general goings-on of the men's retreat last year, but I did have a few additional questions I didn't think to ask him."

"Such as?"

"Did you know before you arrived at the retreat that it was anything more than the power building seminar it was touted to be?"

"No. Stan is the one who talked me into the whole thing in the first place. Initially, I really wasn't interested, but he said that he'd attended a seminar put on by these same folks a year or so ago and that it had really helped him. He was a good guy and, quite honestly, one of my better customers, so I eventually decided to go. I had no idea what I was getting into until after we arrived." He paused briefly and then continued. "Things seemed normal at first, but then some of the guys disappeared. When we found out where they'd gone off to and what they were doing, I was shocked. When I saw all that food just sitting out on a table without a gatekeeper to tell me not to eat it, I went a little crazy. Months and months of nothing other than clean eating had turned me into a glutton of the first degree. I'm lucky I didn't have another heart attack."

"Did you hear from Evagrius Industries after that week?" I asked.

He shook his head. "No. What I did was come home, come clean to my wife, and then swear I was all veggies all the way from that point forward." He stuck out his chest. "I've lost fifty pounds since I returned from that retreat, so I guess it did do me some good in the long run."

"I guess it did," I agreed.

Don didn't seem like the sort to be a blackmail victim. His "sin" was food, and he'd come clean to his wife, so perhaps since he wasn't a blackmail target, he wouldn't be a target for the killer either. Of course, it was entirely possible that I was barking up the wrong tree, and the killer was currently out there stalking victim number four as we spoke.

"Neither Kurt nor Lance are answering their cells," Noah said. "I guess I can try Lance's wife."

"Just call her and say something about wanting to do some remodeling at the church. Ask if she knows how you can get ahold of Lance to talk to him about it, but don't say anything more than that. I'm going to try Colt again."

Colt answered his cell phone this time. I briefly explained what Noah and I were doing and why, and he shared with me that he'd chased down a lead that had ended up being a dead-end but would be back at his office in about thirty minutes. I promised to meet him there once Noah and I had finished speaking to whoever we could get ahold of, and he'd taken me back to my car.

"Lance's wife said he's on an out-of-state job and won't be home for two weeks," Noah shared.

"Okay, then he should be safe for now. I guess, take me back to my car. I'm going to meet up with Colt in a while."

"Did he figure out who's been killing these men?"

"Not yet, but he will."

Chapter 10

By the time I made it back to Colt's office, he'd returned. He was on the phone when I walked in, so I headed toward the ladies' room to freshen up. When I returned to his office, he was jotting notes down on a yellow legal pad.

"So tell me about your afternoon," I jumped in.

"You first. You mentioned on the phone that you'd identified seven men in all who'd attended the men's retreat sponsored by Evagrius Industries last year and that you'd spoken to two of the four men who are still alive."

I nodded. "Travis Kubel and Don Perry have been warned. Both men are heading out of town with their families. Lance Rivers is already out of town on a job and won't be home for two weeks. That just leaves

Kurt Steadman. Noah's tried calling him a couple of times, but he isn't picking up. Apparently, he was fired from his job a while back, and he spends most of his time in bars."

"I can verify that," Colt said. "I've been called in to escort the man home on a few occasions as of late." He paused. "I would like to talk to him since he really might be in danger. I know of a couple bars he prefers to frequent. I'll make some calls and see if I can track him down. Did you learn anything else?"

"Other than what I already told you on the phone, no. We learned that all three of our current victims were linked by making payments to Evagrius Industries, and I wonder if there are other Holiday Bay residents who are likewise linked to this particular company. Just because they didn't attend the retreat with the group from Noah's church doesn't mean they didn't attend the retreat. Travis said there were around a hundred men there from all over the state."

"That's a good question."

"I thought I might call Genevieve and ask her if she can track down a list of anyone who might have made payments to the company and then cross-reference that list with men who live in or near Holiday Bay. Sydney did give me her private number, and she did encourage me to call anytime."

Colt shrugged. "I suppose it doesn't hurt to ask. You call Genevieve, and I'll call around and see if I can track down Kurt."

I took my cell phone into the empty reception area and made my call.

"Go for Gen."

"Genevieve. My name is Abby Sullivan."

"Syd's friend. What can I do for you, Abby Sullivan?"

"I'm calling with a follow-up question to the information you provided to Sydney this morning. I wondered if you could tell me if there are any other men making payments to Evagrius Industries who live in or near Holiday Bay."

"There are seven in all."

Wow. That was fast.

"The three Sydney mentioned to me this morning plus Barnaby Johnson, Clark Havilyn, Ted Newberry, and Robert Jones."

"So Travis Kubel, Don Perry, Lance Rivers, and Kurt Steadman were not making payments to this company?"

"No. Not using those names at least."

"Are Travis Kubel, Don Perry, Lance Rivers, or Kurt Steadman linked to the proposed development south of town?" I asked.

"Hang on."

I could hear typing in the background. "I ran a quick check, and none of those names came up. I can dig deeper and call you back."

"What about Barnaby Johnson, Clark Havilyn, Ted Newberry, and Robert Jones. Are any of these men linked to the proposed development south of town?"

"Hang on."

Again, I heard typing in the background.

"Again, not that I can tell. It looks like out of all the names you've provided to me so far, it's only Oliver Halifax, Henry Goodman, and Stan Fairfield who are linked to the development, the church, the retreat, and payments made to Evagrius Industries. The only link I can find between Barnaby, Clark, Ted, and Robert to the three murder victims are the payments to Evagrius Industries."

"Are Barnaby, Clark, Ted, and Robert linked to each other? Do they attend the same church?"

"Hang on. I'll take a quick look around."

I nibbled on a thumbnail while I waited. It seemed that Genevieve really did know her stuff. It wasn't that she was coming up with anything top secret, but she was fast. Very, very fast.

"No. The four men don't attend the same church. Barnaby attends the Baptist church on South Avenue, Ted and Robert attend the Presbyterian church on Easter Boulevard, and I don't see anything relating to a church on Clark's profile." She paused. "Oh, wait. Clark does occasionally attend the Lutheran church on Seaside Avenue."

"Okay, this has all been very helpful. I really want to thank you for all your help. We wouldn't be nearly as far along as we are without the information you provided."

"No problem. I like to do what I can, and Syd seems to think you're one of the good guys."

With that, she hung up. No goodbye, nothing. Just click and done.

I headed back to Colt's office. I hoped he'd had luck tracking down Kurt. Based on my conversation with Genevieve, it sounded like we might want to track down Barnaby Johnson, Clark Havilyn, Ted Newberry, and Robert Jones, even though payments to Evagrius Industries were the only link the men had to the three current victims. I supposed the killer could be using men who attended the wild party week as the pool from which to draw victims, and given the notes left in the clams that seemed to be the best fit, but my intuition told me there might be more going on than we were currently aware of.

"Any luck with Kurt?" I asked Colt when I arrived at his office.

"No. I called all the bars where I've been called in to pick Kurt up over the past few months, and he isn't at any of them. I also tried his cell phone again, but he didn't pick up."

"And his wife still hasn't returned your call?"

"No. Not yet. How'd you do?"

"I eliminated most of the possible links I had in my mind, but I do have four more names. Barnaby Johnson, Clark Havilyn, Ted Newberry, and Robert Jones are all making payments to Evagrius Industries.

They don't all attend the same church, so I didn't pick up a link there, and Genevieve couldn't find a link between any of the four men to the proposed development south of town. I'm not sure if the payments to Evagrius Industries should place them on the list of possible victims, but I figure it won't hurt to talk to the men. I keep thinking that the payments these men are making to the company are part of some sort of blackmail scheme."

"If the company is luring men to these party weeks and then blackmailing them, why weren't all seven men from Noah's church blackmailed?"

I shrugged. "Maybe they only go after men of affluence. Oliver, Henry, and Stan were in a totally different income class than Travis, Don, Lance, and Kurt. Plus, it sounds like all Lance did was sleep. That's not the sort of thing you'd blackmail someone for doing. And while Don wasn't supposed to eat all that food, overeating isn't the sort of thing to ruin a marriage or chase away customers like Stan with his infidelity and Oliver with his gambling problem. The only one of the remaining four who really seemed to get into any trouble was Kurt. I guess we can ask him if Evagrius Industries contacted him after that week. I suppose he might have been but chose not to pay up. Either that or he made the payments in such a manner that Genevieve couldn't find them in her initial search."

Colt stood, staring at the clock on the wall. It looked as if he was watching the second hand while he tried to make up his mind about something. "Given the fact that our killer might be out there stalking victim number four, I feel like I should be doing more than I am. Tracking down every possible victim we can think of so they can be warned is worthwhile but time-consuming. We aren't even sure at this point how the killer is choosing his victims. We have a couple theories, and I will admit the theories we've come up with do hold water, but for all we know, all we've accomplished by warning potential victims is a temporary reprieve while the killer selects a new victim."

"I get what you're saying. The only way to stop this guy is to catch this guy. The question is, how do we do that?"

Colt seemed to come to a decision. "I know that none of the bodies were found in the victims' homes and, according to the guys from the county who initially searched the homes, there was no sign that the killer had ever been there or that the actual killing took place within the home, but I feel like there might be something they missed. I'm going to head over to the home of each of the three victims we currently have and look around."

"Will anyone be there?" I wondered.

"Oliver's wife is still on her cruise, so I expect the house to be unoccupied except for the live-in maid. I spoke to her yesterday and will call and let her know that I'll be by to take a second look today. Henry is single, so I expect his home will be uninhabited, but I know the next-door neighbor has a key, so I'll call and arrange to have him meet me and let me in. And Stan's wife seems to be out of town, which means his residence will most likely be unoccupied as well. I don't have a key, so I guess I'll see what I can do when I get there."

"I'll go with you," I offered. "Two sets of eyes are better than one."

Chapter 11

Colt managed to get ahold of Oliver's maid, who was happy to let him in, so we headed toward Oliver's home first. His huge estate, perched right on the sea, gave evidence to how well he'd done for himself throughout his career. I didn't have all the specifics but based on what I'd heard from others, Oliver had been an aggressive investor who not only made a lot of money for himself but for his clients as well. The fact that Oliver had been wrapped up in the proposed development wasn't surprising. If there was a hot new investment to be made, he had been the sort to want to make it. The fact that he'd taken things one step further and actually run for town council in an attempt to defeat Dennis Painter and take over his seat really wasn't surprising either. A little research revealed that Dennis seemed to have planned to vote no on the project, so along with Evelyn Child and

Sonya Greenly, they should have been able to send Blaine Holleran and his planned development packing. If Oliver had invested not only his money but the money of his clients as well, it made sense that he would have wanted to do whatever was necessary to push the project through. Of course, in my opinion, if Oliver had chosen to vote on the project rather than abstaining, it would have been a huge conflict of interest. I supposed Oliver just figured he'd find a way to steal the election and then worry about the conflict later.

When we arrived at the estate, Colt knocked on the door, and I stood quietly to his left as we waited for the maid to answer. She was a tall woman with dark hair and a friendly smile.

"Police Chief Wilder. Please come in." She stepped aside.

"Thank you, Collette. This is Abby Sullivan. She's going to walk through with me if that's okay."

"If you want her with you, that's fine with me. Has there been any news? I keep hoping I'll hear that they found the terrible person who did this."

"We don't have a suspect yet, but we're working on it. The reason we wanted to take a second look around was to see if something might pop now that we have additional information."

"Well, look as long as you need to. I'll be in the kitchen, so if you need something, just holler."

"Thank you," Colt said. "I think we'll start in the home office and then take a quick look around the master bedroom. We shouldn't be too long."

Colt had obviously been to the house before since he knew right where to go to find the office.

"Do you have any idea what we're looking for?" I asked.

"I'm not sure. I just hope that if there is something to find, it will jump out at us. Unfortunately, the computer is password protected, and the file cabinet is locked. The guys from the county took the computer but decided not to break into the file cabinet."

I wandered over to the desk. "It looks like Oliver had an old fashion desk calendar." I flipped through the pages. "I didn't know they even made these any longer. It seems that everyone I know uses the calendar on their cell phone."

"There are those who feel they remember things better if they write them down."

"It looks like the page corresponding to the date Oliver's body was found has been left blank, but if you thumb back through a week, there's a notation in the margin of that date that says SF-6/22. June twenty-second was Tuesday. Tuesday was the day we found Oliver's body on the island."

Colt narrowed his gaze. "I do remember that Oliver was heading out to meet with someone when he was last seen. I suppose the person he was meeting was SF."

"Might SF be Stan Fairfield?"

"I guess it could be, but if Oliver was heading out to meet with Stan Fairfield and we assume the person he was meeting with is the person who killed him, then who killed Stan? It seems unlikely SF stands for Stan Fairfield. Of course, without more information, we'll never be able to figure it out."

Colt headed toward the closet. He opened it and began sifting through the items contained within. The desk drawers simply held supplies such as pens and notepads as well as file folders and paperclips. The file cabinets were still locked up tight. I supposed someone might need to take the initiative to break into them at some point. Doing so might require a warrant, but I wasn't sure of that in this situation.

"Check this out," I said after I'd moved from the desk to an unlocked cabinet on the far wall where I'd found blueprints for the proposed resort. The thing really was a monstrosity. Much too large for our isolated stretch of coastline. I had to wonder where the developer thought he was going to find enough employees to fill all the positions he was likely to have. I also wondered how the seven restaurants planned for the property would affect the local eateries, and for the first time, I stopped to wonder how the two hundred rooms and cottages would affect my business.

"Halifax must have been part of the inner circle to have these plans before anyone else," Colt said, studying the large sheet of paper I'd unrolled after taking it from the cabinet. "I know there's a link between the three victims and Evagrius Industries, and given the nature of the crime scenes, that seems to be a good clue, but in the end, I sort of feel like it's going to come back to the resort, which, if you remember, is exactly where we started."

"I agree. If the men were being blackmailed, it seems they were paying up since money is flowing from their accounts into Evagrius Industries' account. I don't see why anyone would have reason to kill them. It seems more likely that the three of them would have gotten together and killed whoever was behind the blackmails."

"Unless that isn't what's going on at all," Colt pointed out. "The blackmail theory is a good one given the entire situation, but the men might have been sending money to Evagrius Industries for another reason. Maybe they were investors. Or perhaps they were paying for a service of some sort."

"Maybe," I agreed. "I guess if we are able to track down the other four men Genevieve told me about who were also making payments to Evagrius Industries, we can ask them why they're making the payments."

Colt frowned as he pulled out his cell. "It's odd that I haven't heard back from any of the men. Kurt is probably drunk and holed up somewhere, but Barnaby, Clark, Ted, and Robert should all be at work."

"Some people don't monitor their phones while they're working. I'm sure once the men get off for the day, they'll call."

Colt took some photos of the office, and then we headed upstairs to the master bedroom. A quick search of the dresser, closet, and nightstands didn't net us any new information, but I did find it interesting that only Oliver's clothes were in this room. I had to wonder if perhaps Mr. and Mrs. Halifax had separate bedrooms. I mentioned my observation to Colt, who decided to ask Collette, who confirmed the couple had kept separate rooms since before she came to work for them. I wasn't sure if that was a relevant piece of information, but it might be something we'd need to know at some point. I supposed it explained why Mrs. Halifax had gone on such a long cruise without her husband.

Colt chatted with Collette for a few minutes, and then we headed down the coastline to the equally magnificent estate owned by Henry Goodman. As Colt had indicated he would, he'd called ahead and had the neighbor meet us with the extra key. As with Oliver's home, it seemed Colt had been here before since once the neighbor let us in, he headed down the hallway to the home office.

"It looks like the computer is gone from here as well."

Colt nodded. "The guys from the county have it. Are the drawers in the desk locked?"

I tried the top middle drawer, and it opened. As with Oliver's desk, this draw held items such as pens, notepads, and paperclips. I tried the top drawer on the right, but it was locked. The bottom drawer on the right contained stacks of file folders, but the folders were empty. It looked as if he had been saving the old file folders to recycle for future use.

The top drawer on the left was locked, and the bottom drawer on the left contained personal items, including a bottle of really good scotch. It felt strange rummaging through the man's personal items, but if there was something to find, it seemed likely that was where I'd find it. The drawer held a pack of gum, two tubes of lip balm, a small bottle of hand lotion, and a package of Hershey's kisses. I guess the guy had a sweet tooth. The drawer also contained a pair of reading glasses, a small address book, and a book of matches. Removing the address book from the drawer, I flipped to the F's. There were at least fifteen entries. Stan Fairfield was one of them. There were two other entries for individuals with a first name that began with S and a last name beginning with F: Sabrina Fox and Steve Farley. Neither name sounded familiar. I supposed they might be friends or clients. The book was old and the cover worn, which led me to believe that the addresses in the book were attached to people Henry had known for a while.

"Do you know Sabrina Fox or Steve Farley?" I asked Colt, who was sorting through a closet.

"No. Why?"

"I found an address book in one of the drawers. I looked for names with the initials SF, and those two came up. I suspect this book might contain addresses and phone numbers for people Henry has known for a while. It's possible the information included is no longer accurate, but it seemed worthwhile to take a peek."

"Let's bring it with us. I'm sure Henry has a more recent contact list in his cell phone, but so far, his cell phone hasn't been found."

"I take it his computer is password protected."

Colt nodded. "The guys at the county office are working on it."

"There's also an entry for someone named Fagen under the F's," I said. "No first name, just Fagen." I flipped back to the S's. "There's an entry for Spades and one for Salvatore. I'm not sure if those are first or last names or maybe businesses."

"Spades is a bar located about thirty miles east of here. I'm not sure about Fagen or Salvatore."

I slipped the little address book into my pocket and worked on trying to open the two locked drawers. There wasn't a place for a key, so the chances were that the drawers could be opened by working a lever. I slipped my hand into the top center drawer and felt around. The center drawer had been open when we arrived, but this drawer did have a place for a key. I supposed that the only way to open the drawers to the side would be to work the latch when the middle drawer was open, which meant if the middle drawer was locked, the top two were secure as well.

"Bingo," I said aloud as I found the latch and popped the locks on the side drawers. The top right drawer contained files that looked to be current in nature. The file on the top held contracts relating to the proposed development. "I found some stuff relating to the proposed development."

"Okay. Let's take those with us. Is there anything else?"

"Some customer files that look current. Maybe we should take them as well. I'm not sure if they're relevant to what happened to Henry, but it wouldn't hurt to look through everything. I wonder who will take over all these escrows. Did Henry have a partner or work in an office with other agents?"

"He did work out of an office, although I don't suppose he spent much time there. I'll take the files over to the real estate office and make sure someone who knows what to do with them takes custody once I've had a chance to look through them." He closed the closet door. "Nothing in here, and the file cabinets are locked."

I opened the top left drawer of the desk, where I found a journal-sized book with a black leather cover, which contained handwritten notes. Lots and lots of handwritten notes. "I might have found something," I said, holding the book up.

"Bring it as well." He glanced at his watch. "I guess I should get back to the office. Maybe one of the half dozen people I left messages for called the office line. I'll make plans to head to Stan's house at another time."

"Where's Peach today?"

"She called in sick. Hopefully, she'll be back tomorrow. I really need her this week."

"It is a bad week for her to be out."

When we arrived back at Colt's office, I asked if he wanted to come by the inn this evening for Georgia's catch of the day dinner, but he said he wanted to stay in town, close to the phone until this case was wrapped up one way or the other. He especially wanted to be close by, knowing that unless something we'd done had given the killer reason to veer from his plan, it was highly likely there would be a fourth victim by the end of the day tomorrow. Of course, the idea that there would be seven victims was just a hunch. It was just as likely that we were wrong about the whole seven deadly sins thing. I really hoped we were and that the three men who'd died would be the only three men to die.

I hated to bail on Colt, but I felt I should make an appearance at Georgia's dinner, so I kissed Colt on the cheek and headed home. When I pulled up in front of the cottage, I noticed Annabelle and Haley playing on the lawn. Stepping out of my car and waving, I headed in that direction.

"Hi, girls. Whatcha doing?"

"Cartwheels," Haley answered.

"We were helping Uncle Jeremy with the pond, but that got boring," Annabelle added.

I looked around the area and then back at Haley. "Is your mom here?"

"No," she answered. "She's with Uncle Rod. I'm going to spend the night with Annabelle."

Uncle Rod? "I see." I glanced toward the inn. "I'm going to head inside. You girls have fun."

I walked back to my car, grabbed my purse from the backseat, and headed inside.

"Oh good, you're back," Georgia said. "I have bread in the oven, and Ramos needs to go out. Would you take him for me?"

"Yeah. No problem. In fact, I'll take both dogs for a short walk." I set my purse on the counter. "I hear that Christy is out with Rod, and Haley is spending the night with Annabelle."

Georgia frowned. "Yeah. I heard. I know it's none of my business, but the whole thing isn't sitting quite right with me." She opened the oven and shuffled the bread pans. "I briefly spoke to Christy when she dropped Haley off, and she insists that she and Rodney are just friends, but when I asked if Noah would be going to dinner with them, she shared that he was busy with bible study this evening and would be unavailable."

I glanced at Ramos, who was prancing around. "I guess it really isn't any of our business, but I agree. The whole thing is sitting wrong with me as well. I have news about the murder victims. I'll fill you in when I get back."

After grabbing two leashes to have just in case they were needed, I called both dogs and set off down the bluff trail. It was a gorgeous day. Sometimes having a dog who needed walking several times a day was a real blessing in that it demanded that you take brief pauses in order to head outdoors and really enjoy all that nature had to offer.

As we neared the bench that overlooked the sea about halfway between our place and Tanner's, I noticed that Joel and Emma sat side by side, seemingly enjoying the view as I'd been.

"Beautiful day," I said, pausing as I neared the bench.

"It really is," Joel agreed. "I think this is one of my new favorite places to sit and share a memory."

"Or a dream," Emma added.

"A dream?" I asked, figuring that if it was a private dream, she could just say as much.

"One of the few things my husband and I disagreed on was travel," Emma shared. "We both loved to get out and about, but Jasper didn't like to fly, so for him, the ultimate trip was a road trip. We had some good ones, and I have to say I've been pretty much everywhere you can drive to, but I always wanted to go to Europe. In my mind, a grand tour involving old buildings, libraries, and museums would have been the ultimate adventure." She turned and glanced at Joel. "Joel has been pretty much everywhere I've ever dreamed of traveling. He's been generous with his time and has spent hours describing each and every site I've dreamed of visiting one day. I doubt I'll ever get there at this point, but it has been nice to travel the world in my imagination."

"I suppose that it's not too late to make the trip," I said.

"That's what I've been telling her," Joel seconded. "Trying to fit everything in might be exhausting, but maybe a shorter trip with longer layovers would provide a sample of the real thing."

"I couldn't go alone," she said. "I've never been anywhere alone other than here. It would be too much to even consider."

"Maybe we could go together," Joel suggested. "I have a buddy I like to travel with, but he's had some medical issues lately and hasn't been up for a trip abroad. I do enjoy traveling with a friend. Maybe we could plan a trip. As friends, of course," he added when she began to frown.

"I guess that might be something to consider," she eventually said. "I really would love to see Rome."

"Rome is lovely, and once you're that far, it wouldn't be too much more effort to travel to France and Spain."

Emma's gaze grew distant. "I'll need to think on it. It sounds wonderful, but..." She let the thought dangle.

I knew how hard it could be to take a step out of your comfort zone and try something new once you'd found a way of being alone after so many years of being one half of a whole.

"I'm sure Joel would be a wonderful tour guide," I added. "Traveling with a seasoned international traveler who's already been where you're going would be a lot easier. Being with someone who knows where to stay and how to get around would make the trip less stressful."

"I guess that's true." She smiled. "It does sound wonderful. I'll have to give it some thought."

I chatted with the pair for a few more minutes, and then the dogs and I turned around and headed back toward the inn. I was sure Georgia would want to be filled in on the investigation, and I was anxious to get her take on things.

"So tell me your news," Georgia said the minute I walked into the inn. "I can't believe you dropped the teaser and then left, and here I was stuck with my bread."

"Sorry. I guess I should have waited to say anything until we got back from our walk."

"So spill. What did you find out?"

I filled her in with all the news I'd picked up since we'd last spoken.

"Wow." Her cheeks had paled. "So, do you think there could be four more victims before this is over?"

"I think there *might* be four more victims before this is over. We still don't actually know anything for certain. Colt is working on it. I know he feels the pressure to figure this out before there's another death. I feel bad for him. I wish I could do more, but this really isn't my area of expertise."

"It was nice of Sydney to do what she could before she left. It must be an unusual sort of life to have a job that keeps you involved with serial killers and gruesome deaths all the time."

"Honestly, I can't imagine doing something like that for a living. Are you still planning to grill the fish tonight?"

"I am. The fish guy dropped off a really great selection, all cleaned and ready to go. Do you think Colt will be by?"

"No. Colt wants to stay close to town until whatever is going to happen does or doesn't happen. If our theory is correct, the next death will occur tomorrow. At this point, I guess all we can do is hope that something we've done today put a kink in those plans, assuming, of course, that we're even on the right track, which at this point isn't a given."

"Once I get the bread out of the oven, I'm going to run next door and change. Nikki will be by to help serve since Jeremy has been working on the pond all day."

"Speaking of that, I wanted to check in with Jeremy. I think I'll do that now."

I headed outside, where the girls were still playing on the grass, and then I walked down the path to where Jeremy was working.

"Wow, you've made so much progress in such a short amount of time," I said as I took in the pond, which had already been lined and filled with water.

"I was motivated to get it done. I just need to hook up the pump for the waterfall, which I plan to do next, and then the hardscape will be done. I'm going to head into town tomorrow to pick up some plants."

"So, in addition to low-lying plants around the edge of the pond, are you going to add plants to the shelves within the pond?"

"That's the idea. We'll need to remove the plants when it gets cold since the pond will freeze, so they'll remain in their containers. I'm going to build a small greenhouse where they can winter. The ferns and other water-loving plants that will be planted around the rim of the pond have been selected based on their ability to withstand the winter conditions and come back strong each spring."

"It sounds like you've really done your research."

"I have. I wanted to be sure I knew exactly what I was getting into before I started."

"Are you going to add fish?" I wondered.

"No. At least not at this point. My goal for this season is to get the plants established and the water balanced and clear. I think there's a learning curve with that." He put his hands on his hips and looked around. "I'm going to add benches for reading and meditating there and there." He pointed to flat shady places that he'd marked off. "The two trees near the pathway are large enough for a hammock, so I thought I'd add one of those as well. It might take a couple seasons before I have the area exactly the way I envision, but I think I have a good start."

"You do, and I'm really impressed. I just hope the construction crew doesn't stomp on your landscaping when they begin building the cottages next spring."

"I'm going to rope off the areas where the more delicate plants will be added and make sure that Lonnie warns his guys to tread lightly." He glanced toward the lawn area that was just out of eyeshot from where we stood. "Did you see the girls when you came through?"

I nodded. "They're playing on the lawn. Haley mentioned that she'll be spending the night."

"Yeah. Christy asked Mylie if she would watch Haley. I guess Noah's busy tonight, so she's going out with Rodney."

"Is Mylie here?"

"She had some work stuff to take care of, but she'll be back by dinner. Annabelle was thrilled to have Haley to play with, so I suggested she leave her here." He looked at his watch. "I guess I should start cleaning up. Oh, before I forget, Lonnie came by earlier. He wanted to talk to you about getting the ground cleared and the foundations poured for the cottages this fall rather than waiting until spring. He figured if the groundwork was done, then his guys could get an earlier start on the rest."

"That makes sense, but I wouldn't want them working when the inn is packed or if we had an event going on. I'll call Lonnie. There might be a window when he can get the groundwork done."

I had to admit that I was really excited about the new cottages. Yes, they were going to be a significant expense, and yes, they were going to require trips to the granite store, flooring store, and paint store, but I'd really enjoyed picking everything out when we'd done the inn, and I was excited to have another project to focus on. I was sure that Georgia and Lacy would be as excited to go along on these little shopping trips as they'd done before. I'd never been into antiquing until I met Lacy, but now the thought of having a reason to seek out unique furniture to restore and display had me feeling excited about the project ahead.

Chapter 12

As it turned out, when I called Lonnie about the cottages, he mentioned that the twins were feeling better and his parents were going to come over and give him and Lacy a break. He'd planned to take his wife out to dinner, but when I mentioned the catch of the day cookout and invited them to attend, he said that Lacy would enjoy an evening with friends after more than a week with no one other than the seven and under crowd to hang out with. Lonnie suggested that the two of us could talk specifics about the project when they arrived, so I headed inside to let Georgia know there would be two more for dinner. I knew Colt would have to skip this evening's event, but Georgia mentioned that Tanner and Nikki would both be there, so it looked like we would have a full house, or in this case, a full lawn and patio area.

"Do you need any help?" I asked Georgia once I'd informed her that the Parkers would be joining us.

"No. I think I have everything under control. Jeremy washed down the patio and all the patio furniture today, and the blue and white flowers he planted look lovely. It's supposed to be another near-perfect evening. I think everyone will have a wonderful time."

"It looks like we can count Rodney out since he's with Christy today. Have you heard from Chris?"

"He's in. In fact, he's here. He only worked a half-day today. I think he might be in the library with Samantha. He had some paperwork to do, and when I'd walked past the library on my way to the stairway, I noticed that she'd joined him. They were smiling and laughing and seemed to be having a good time."

"That's good. Getting over someone is hard. I'm glad Samantha's enjoying her stay with us." I glanced toward the back door. It looks like Lonnie and Lacy are here. I'm going to grab Lonnie while I can so we can go over his plans. I'll send Lacy in to chat with you. I'm sure she'd enjoy a glass of wine and some adult conversation."

I arrived at the clearing where Georgia, Jeremy, and I usually parked, and Lonnie had chosen to park as well. I hugged Lacy and told her Georgia had a glass of wine with her name on it, and she headed in that direction. I then suggested to Lonnie that we go over whatever he wanted to go over before everyone began gathering on the patio.

"I guess Jeremy told you that I hoped to get the groundwork done, and the foundations poured before the first snow. If we don't get the foundations in, we'll need to wait for the ground to thaw and dry out next spring before we can get started. Depending on the sort of spring we have, that could push us into May, but if the foundations are in, we can start the framing as soon as the snow melts. There have been some years when we've able to get started as early as March."

"Okay. I like your idea in theory. We're totally booked until Labor Day, and then we're mostly booked from October through December. There is a window after Labor Day through around October first when we might be able to work it out for you to bring in crews and equipment during the week. I'll need to verify our current reservations with Georgia. The last thing I want to do is have backhoes and work crews stirring up dust and making a lot of noise when we have an inn full of guests."

"If you can get me some dates, I'll line up as many men as I can get and try to get all four pads laid in as quickly as possible."

"Do you think slab foundations are the way to go? The inn has a crawl space. So does my cottage, for that matter."

"We could do pillars if you prefer. We'll still need to prepare the ground and install the pillars this fall, but it would make for a little less mess. What I'd probably do is clear and level the land, install the pillars and then go ahead and take care of the crossbeams. We'll need to cover everything to protect it from the elements, but I can have my guys lay down tarps."

"Okay, let's talk to Georgia and pencil in some dates that might work. As far as which type of foundation we should have, I'll let you decide. Is there anything else you need to figure out?"

He nodded. "The architect sent over several drawings. We'll need to make some choices. Whichever foundation we decide on, we'll need to have the footprint set in stone before we start. I guess the biggest question is whether you decided on one or two bedrooms or a combination of both."

I licked my lips. "I have been thinking about that. On the one hand, two-bedroom cottages would be attractive for families. On the other hand, I worry about attracting too many children and altering the peaceful and quiet setting we currently enjoy. We don't have a policy against children, and there are families who check in from time to time, but since the suites are only one bedroom, families don't necessarily think to book with us."

"I have six kids, so I get what you're saying. It would be a shame to destroy the peaceful setting you have here. Let's take a walk and look at the sites. Maybe we can narrow things down a bit."

"Okay, that sounds good. Jeremy has been working on the pond all week. You'll want to see that anyway. It's a lot larger than I thought it would be, but when coupled with the waterfall trickling into it, I can see that once he gets the plants in, it's going to be a favorite place to while away a summer afternoon."

"It was a good idea to place it back in that grove of mature trees so there will be lots of shade. I'm planning to place the two pond-side cottages in such a way so as to preserve as many trees as possible. If we're creative, we might get away without taking any of them out."

"That would be wonderful."

Once Lonnie and I arrived at the pond, we walked around the area, discussing the exact placement for two of the cottages. A two-bedroom unit would be bigger and harder to tuck away without disturbing the grove, so in my mind, that helped me to decide on one-bedroom units, at least for these two cottages. Lonnie positioned our bodies so I could get a feel for different frontages. I knew I wanted the cottages to have covered porches and that I didn't want the cottages directly facing each other. We decided that placing them both on the western edge of the pond and angling them toward the pond so that when you were sitting on the porch or in the living area, you were looking at the waterfall and not your neighbor's front door was the way to go.

We also discussed landscaping tricks that would provide screens and act as privacy barriers, and we discussed the placement of the gas fireplaces and the outdoor grills we planned to install for all the cottages.

Georgia, Jeremy, and I had discussed the fact that winters could be hard, so we planned to offer the cottages from May through October. Jeremy would break down the pond and winterize the cottages each November after the Halloween crowd cleared out.

Since we might want to look at year-round cottages someday, I wanted them insulated enough for use in the winter if we chose, but in the beginning, having seasonal cottages just seemed like the right decision.

Once Lonnie and I had finished talking about the details relating to the two pond cottages, we headed to the piece of land reserved for the ocean-front cottage. Again, we decided on a one-bedroom unit with a wall of windows overlooking the sea. We placed a gas fireplace in the corner, and we angled the bedroom so that it overlooked the sea as well.

The fourth cottage was tucked away at the very western border of the property. It had a partial ocean view and was well away from the inn and the other cottages. I decided to make this one a two-bedroom. Couples with children would be attracted to the two-bedroom unit and would have plenty of room to stretch out. While the cottage was pretty isolated at this point, two of the additional four cottages that had been drawn onto the property for future development, should we choose, were slated to be built along this western border as well.

"Have you figured out the meal issue?" Lonnie asked as we walked back toward the inn. Meals were eaten in the dining room or on the patio during the summer. Even when we were fully booked, there was plenty of room for all the guests to eat together. With the addition of the cottages, accommodating everyone for a communal meal would be tricky when the place was fully booked.

"Georgia and I are working on it. It won't be so bad when the weather is good, since most guests choose to eat outside anyway and we have plenty of room on the patio. The cottages will only be offered late spring through mid-fall, so we won't have to worry about meal times in the winter. If we have a fully booked inn while it's still too cold to eat outdoors, I guess we may have to offer A and B meal times. At least for dinner. Breakfast is served buffet-style, and folks tend to wander in at different times anyway."

"It's good that you're just starting with four cottages instead of doing all eight right off the bat. It will give you time to work out any issues that arise from the extra guests, and it will allow you more time to decide if eight might be more than you want to deal with."

"I agree. I really want to thank you for all your help. You've had a lot of great ideas."

"Just part of the Lonnie Parker Construction package." He smiled.

Lonnie headed over to join Tanner at the grill, and I headed inside to see what Georgia and Lacy were doing. I was sorry Colt was going to miss the event. He would have enjoyed getting together with friends.

"Oh good, you're back," Lacy said when I walked into the kitchen. "Georgia has been filling me in on Holiday Bay's murder spree."

"You hadn't heard?" I asked.

"I heard that Oliver Halifax was found dead. I heard that most folks figured that his death had something to do with the proposed development and his involvement with the developer and the town council. I heard that Henry Goodman was found dead the following day. He's also involved with the proposed development, so I figured the two deaths were linked to that. But I've been knee-deep in sick kids and hadn't heard about Stan Fairfield's death or the whole thing with the men's party week. I can't believe three men are dead, nor can I believe that seven men from our church went on this wicked week event while pretending to be away at a men's wealth and power retreat."

"I don't think Travis, Don, Lance, and Kurt knew what they were getting into before they arrived," I said. "I know Stan recruited everyone, so he knew what was really going on, and it seemed that Oliver and Henry might have known as well."

"Henry is single. He can do whatever he wants, and there's no one who's going to care about it. Why would he bother with a week like that? Henry has cash. If he wanted to let loose, why wouldn't he just head to Atlantic City for the week?" Lacy asked.

"I don't know," I admitted. "Stan is a married man and a respected dentist in the community. If he wanted to spend a few days with hot and cold running women, I could see how he might get lured into something like that. And Oliver clearly has a gambling problem, yet he invests other people's money. I can see why Oliver might not want news of his addiction getting around. But I'm not sure how Henry fits into all this, and I'm not sure how this retreat led to the deaths of three men, but that is the way it's looking."

Lacy wrinkled her nose. "I wouldn't be so sure about that. Even after Georgia shared news of the wild weeklong retreat put on by Evagrius Industries with me, I still think the motive behind the deaths might be the proposed development. People who live in the area, especially those who have lived here for a long time, have strong opinions on both sides of the conflict. Lines are being drawn. Neighbors who used to have cookouts together are no longer speaking. My hairdresser told me that she and her sister got into a huge fight over it, and they are seriously on the outs. I know you're relatively new to the area, so you might not be picking up on the level of tension the way I am."

"Okay. Say that's true. Let's say that the proposed development is at the heart of the murders. Who would want to stop the development bad enough that they'd kill three people over it, and how do the notes in the clams fit into it?"

"It does seem that whoever is behind this knew about the wild week even if it wasn't the motive for murder." Lacy pursed her lips. "You said Travis Kubel, Don Perry, Lance Rivers, and Kurt Steadman went to the retreat with the three murder victims."

I nodded.

"Travis has been very outspoken about his opposition to the proposed development. He even led a protest outside the town hall during the last town council meeting. I think Travis might be angry enough over what he refers to as the murder of our small town to have killed three men, but he doesn't strike me as the sort who would actually become violent. He actually seems like a pretty nice guy. I would probably go so far as to say that he might have even imagined doing something violent to save the town he loves, but I would be shocked if he methodically killed three men."

I had to agree with Lacy. I hadn't picked up the killer vibe when we spoke to Travis, and he seemed genuinely concerned that he might be a target. I supposed that might have been an act, but his fear seemed genuine. "And the others?" I asked.

"Don Perry is not a physically strong man. He opposes the new development, but he doesn't seem to be as wrapped up in it as Travis is. Based on what I've been told, it sounds like the killer got up close to these men, stabbed them with a hypodermic needle, and then moved them to the site where they were found after they died. I don't think Don could have physically moved these men. At least, not without help. And if he did have help, who helped him?"

"And Lance?" I asked.

"Lance favors the project. I think he figures there will be a lot of construction work available if a project such as the proposed development is approved. I can't see him as having a motive to kill the men who all clearly supported the approval of the development. As for Kurt..." She paused before continuing. "I'm not sure. Kurt is a hothead, especially when he drinks. I can totally see him getting mad over something and becoming violent. I'm not sure how he felt about the proposed project, but he does have deep-rooted anger issues. The thing is, his anger seems to be explosive. I just can't see him as being the sort to carry out a very methodically executed murder like the ones carried out this week. If these men had been shot and left for dead or stabbed in an alley, sure, I'd believe Kurt could be behind the deaths, but killing someone by injection and then going to all the trouble to move and pose them? I don't think so."

"Okay, so if the proposed development is the motive, who do you think did it?" I asked. "Who was enraged enough about what the resort would do to the town to kill three men? Who would have used the clams and the notes as diversions?"

She paused and thought about it. She tapped her chin and sipped her wine while she thought. It occurred to me that perhaps I should have thought to speak to Lonnie and Lacy earlier. They had both lived in Holiday Bay forever, but it had been a crazy couple of days, and I hadn't thought about it.

"Probably the most outspoken opponent to the proposed development is Daryl White. Daryl is the president of the local lodging association, which I guess you must know since as a lodging property owner, you're most likely a member of the association."

"I am," I confirmed. "Although I've never actually attended any meetings."

"I have," Georgia said. "I know Daryl, and I agree that he's not at all happy that the town council has agreed to look at the project. Still, he doesn't seem like the sort to kill anyone."

"I agree," Lacy said. "I'm just listing names at this point, and if we're looking at a list of men and women who oppose the project, Daryl would have to be at the top of the list. The second person on the list would probably be Justin Brentwood, followed by Barnaby Johnson."

"Wait!" I said. "Barnaby Johnson was on the list Genevieve gave me of men making payments to Evagrius Industries. I'm not sure that fact is important at this point, but it sounds as if this man is both opposed to the project and familiar with the retreats thrown by Evagrius Industries."

"Is Barnaby the sort who would kill three men over something like a disruption to his lifestyle?" Georgia asked.

Lacy didn't answer right away. When she did, she indicated that Barnaby might actually make a pretty good suspect.

"Barnaby is a very rigid man. He has definite ideas about right and wrong, and he tends to view the world as a pretty black and white place. Barnaby's extremely conservative and isn't the sort who is tolerant of the ideas of others. He's the sort to judge those he comes into contact with, although I can sort of see him getting mixed up in one of those fantasy retreats. I can also see him wanting to hide it if he did. He would consider his involvement to be a sin of the biggest sort and wouldn't want anyone else to know about his indiscretion."

"Which would explain the payments to Evagrius Industries," I said. "We've speculated from the beginning that the company might lure men out to their site with the promise of a power building retreat, only to provide a very different option once they arrived. It didn't sound as if the men were forced to partake of the options provided, and many didn't, but it seems that those who did give in to temptation might have had to pay the company to keep things quiet."

"If we find out that exact thing happened to Barnaby, I won't be at all surprised."

"So does it seem as if this man would be physically able to kill and move the men who died?" I asked, having never met the man.

Lacy nodded. "Barnaby is a large man. Six two. Two fifty. He could have killed and easily moved the men. And he was a medic in the Army, so he'd know how to use drugs to kill a man."

"It sounds like this man might be the person we're looking for," I said. "I need to call Colt. He may have already spoken to Barnaby, but if he hasn't, I think he'll want to."

Chapter 13

I'd shared the conversation I'd had with Lacy with Colt, who agreed that Barnaby made a good suspect. He'd been trying to get ahold of him ever since I'd left, but at that point, he hadn't had any luck. Colt still hadn't tracked down Kurt by late yesterday but had managed to talk to and clear Clark Havilyn, Ted Newberry, and Robert Jones. He was going to keep trying to track down both Barnaby and Kurt. He'd promised to call me later that evening, but he never did, so I figured I'd call him this morning.

I wondered if he'd even gone home. When I'd left his office, he had the files and books we'd discovered that afternoon to look through, plus he planned to take a closer look at the phone and bank records of all the victims. I knew the possibility of a fourth victim was weighing heavy on his mind. It was weighing heavy on my mind as well. It was a little like being in a room with a ticking bomb. You could hear it ticking down the minutes and knew it would eventually explode, but you didn't know when or how severe it would be.

I was about to call Colt's number when my cell phone rang.

"Sydney?"

"Hi, Abby. I hope it isn't too early."

"Not for me, but I'm three hours later than you are on the West Coast. It must be five a.m. there."

"It is, but I'm up and heading out to work. I figured I wouldn't have time to make personal calls once I got there and wanted to check in with you. Did you find your killer?"

"No. Not yet, but we have made progress." I'd spent the next fifteen minutes catching her up. "How are you doing with your killer?" I asked after telling her everything I'd learned about our killer since she'd left.

"I spent some time with my team yesterday when I got back to the West Coast. I feel like we're getting close, although we aren't quite there yet."

"I guess these things take time."

She sighed. "They do. It's frustrating to wait for the clues to come together when you know that someone else might die before you can figure it out."

"Tell me about it. I was just thinking the same thing. If we have a fourth victim, it will likely be today. I feel like my skin is crawling with anxiety, but there really isn't a lot I can do that I haven't already done."

"It's not your job to catch this guy. It's Colt's, and I can tell that he's a good cop. He'll figure it out."

"Yeah, I think so too. By the way, I called and spoke to Genevieve yesterday. I wanted her to track down some additional information. She's so fast and so nice. She didn't seem at all put out that I was taking up her time."

"Gen is a super nice person. She quit the NSA to work for Ezra because she isn't a fan of rules and constraints, but in the end, Gen really just wants to catch the bad guy and is always willing to help if she can. She'll be a good ally for you. I call her all the time, and she's always happy to help when she can."

"That's good to know. Colt and I both really appreciate all the help you've provided."

"I was happy to help and sorry I couldn't stay longer."

We chatted for a while longer, but then she had to leave for work, and I wanted to call Colt, so we said goodbye and promised to stay in touch.

My call to Colt went directly to his voicemail. I left him a message, suggesting lunch if he had time, and then I headed over to the inn to say hi to our guests and check in with Georgia. With the clam bake tomorrow, it was likely she'd have errands for me to run, which I'd gladly do. Since there didn't seem to be anything I could do to help Colt with his investigation, I was happy to stay busy.

I noticed Samantha and Chris sitting on the patio, sipping mugs of coffee before I ever reached the inn, so I changed course and headed in their direction.

"Good morning," I said.

"Hey, Abby." Samantha smiled.

I had to admit she looked happier and a lot more relaxed than she had when she'd first arrived.

"Chris and I are just sitting here talking about the clam bake on the island tomorrow. Is it still on? We heard about the murder victim you found and weren't sure how that would all play out."

"As of now, the clam bake is still on. The man who died was killed elsewhere, and the police determined there were no additional clues to find on the island, so we have the go-ahead to hold the event."

"I was sorry to hear that a man died, but happy the event won't be canceled," Samantha said. "I've been looking forward to it."

"It should be a good time. In addition to the delicious food Georgia has planned, we have the murder mystery, which is always fun. Be sure to get to the marina early. We have a boat that will ferry guests over, but I expect that a line will form before we're able to get everyone across."

"We both planned to head over on the first shuttle," Samantha confirmed.

"I thought about taking my boat over, but Georgia said there wouldn't be anywhere to tie up," Chris added.

"That's true. There's only one dock, and the boats we hired will be going back and forth all afternoon and evening, so tying up and staying won't be possible." I glanced toward the inn. "I guess I'll head in and check in with Georgia. You both enjoy this absolutely perfect morning."

"Oh, we will," Samantha promised.

Georgia was busy in the kitchen, Joel and Emma were deep in conversation, and it seemed that Rodney hadn't returned to the inn last night, so I decided to get ready and head into town. If Colt hadn't called me back by the time I got into town, I'd stop by his office and see if Peach could help me track him down.

As it turned out, no one was at Colt's office when I arrived. Since the door was locked up tight, I called and left yet another message on Colt's cell phone and then headed to the rental shop to pick up the items Georgia had reserved for tomorrow night. If Colt still hadn't called by the time I finished there, maybe I'd try his house. It really wasn't like him to not call me back even if he was busy. I thought about the last time I'd been unable to contact him. In that instance, he'd been badly injured, so not being able to make contact with him now was bringing up all sorts of insecurities.

After I'd picked up the items from the rental shop, I decided to head over to Velma's for coffee. Maybe she knew where Colt was. He had breakfast with her almost every morning that he didn't have breakfast with me.

"Lacy," I greeted my friend after noticing her sitting at the counter, chatting with Velma. "I didn't expect to see you here. I guess the twins must be doing better."

"They are. Of course, this is the hard part where they feel much better and want to play but still aren't allowed to go outside or overdo it. Lonnie stayed home with them so I could run some necessary errands. I suppose coffee with Velma isn't an absolutely necessary errand, but then again, it did seem necessary for my sanity."

I sat down on the stool next to her. "If it helps, I never saw you here."

Lacy laughed. "Lonnie won't mind that I made the stop. He wants me sane and knows this will help." She nodded her head toward the back of the room. "Look who's here."

I noticed a man sitting alone in a booth. "Who?"

"Barnaby Johnson."

I turned a little, so I had a better view of the man who had finished his meal and was sorting through his wallet for cash to pay his bill. "Colt has been trying to track him down. I'm not sure if he was ever successful. I've been calling Colt all morning, but he isn't picking up, and he isn't calling me back."

"That's odd," Lacy said.

"Did you leave a message?" Velma asked.

I nodded. "I hope Colt simply misplaced his cell phone or let the battery run down or something like that." I glanced at Velma. "I actually stopped in to see if you'd seen him."

"No. I haven't seen Colt since yesterday."

"He's getting up," I said.

The man had dropped his money on the table and had gotten up to leave.

"I'm going to follow him." I looked at Velma. "Try to track Colt down. Tell him to call me."

I stood up as the man exited the diner. Lacy stood up next to me. "I'm coming with you."

I hesitated and then nodded. By the time we made it to my car, Barnaby had a head start.

"He made a left onto Pine Avenue," Lacy said from the passenger seat next to me.

I sped up just a bit.

"Don't get too close. He'll see us," Lacy warned.

"I know how to tail someone."

"Really?" She crossed her arms over her chest. "Are you a cop?"

"No, but I write about cops tailing suspects all the time. The trick is to hang back but not so far back so that you lose them."

"He just made a right onto the highway," Lacy said.

I turned on my turn signal and followed. I hoped the guy wasn't paying all that much attention to his surroundings since there weren't a lot of cars on the highway to hide behind.

"I think he's going to pull onto Hanover Lane. There are a few houses out there, and I sort of remember that he lives out that way," Lacy pointed to the truck in front of us.

"I'm going to make the turn, but if he pulls into a drive, we'll continue on by and park down the road. We'll walk back. Try calling Colt again."

Lacy did as I asked. As we expected, Barnaby pulled onto a dirt drive leading out to an isolated house. I drove past and then pulled onto a side road. I found a clearing and parked.

"So what now?" Lacy asked. "Do we just wait until Colt calls back?"

"I want to get a look inside the house." I grabbed my door handle.

"You're going up to the house? Are you crazy?"

"I'm not going to knock on the door or anything like that. I'm just going to sneak up to the house and peek in a window or two. I feel like we need to know what we're dealing with just in case Colt doesn't call back."

"What we should do is call 911. If Colt isn't available and Peach isn't in the office, it will ring through to the county office."

"And what are we going to tell them?" I asked. "So far, we haven't actually seen Barnaby do anything other than have breakfast in town. Colt wanted to talk to him because of his connection to Evagrius Industries, but we don't know that he actually did anything wrong, and we certainly don't know that whatever is going on can be classified as an emergency. I think we need to take a peek and then decide what to do."

Lacy blew out a breath. "Okay, but I want to go on record and say that I don't like this."

"You can wait here," I suggested.

"No. If you're going, then I'm going."

I locked my car, and then Lacy and I headed down the road. When we got to the driveway Barnaby had turned onto, we headed into the woods, which provided a bit of cover. Once we reached the back of the house, we slowly tip-toed our way to one of the back windows and looked inside. No one was in the room. It looked to be a spare bedroom. The room was much like any other room, but the thing that made me gasp was a pile of plastic clams like those found with the three victims lying on the bed. I'd just opened my mouth when a large hand clamped onto my face from behind. I felt a moment of panic before I realized it was Colt's voice whispering in my ear. I glanced next to me to see that Colt's other hand was over Lacy's mouth. She looked as terrified as I felt.

"I'm going to remove my hands," Colt said into our ears. "You need to be quiet. Understand?"

I nodded. Lacy must have nodded as well since he removed his hands from our faces, grabbed us each by the hand, and dragged us into the woods. Once we were well away from the house, he demanded to know what we were thinking following a suspected killer to an isolated house.

"It was Abby's idea," Lacy said, throwing me under the bus.

I scowled at her. "I guess it was my idea. But I knew you'd been trying to track this guy down, and I didn't know if he was going home. I didn't want him to disappear again. I tried to call you a bunch of times, but you never answered, and you never returned my calls."

"I seem to have lost my cell phone. I think it fell out of my pocket at the crime scene."

"Crime scene?"

"Kurt Steadman is dead. Same as the others."

Wow, I hated to hear that. "There's a pile of those plastic clams on the bed in the spare bedroom," I said. "Barnaby has to be the killer."

"Yeah. I think he is, which is why I'm here. There was a note in Kurt's pocket about a meeting with Barnaby early this morning. The county guys are on the way. I'm going to wait here to make sure that Barnaby doesn't decide to leave before backup gets here. The two of you are to return to your car and wait for me."

"Okay," I said, wishing I could wait with Colt but not wanting to push it. He already looked sort of mad.

"Lacy and I will wait in the car. It's parked down on the next dirt road to the north that veers off to the right."

Lacy and I had made it back to my car, and I was just unlocking the doors and preparing to get in when I heard a shot that was quickly followed by another shot.

"Colt!" I took off running. I could hear Lacy calling to me as I ran faster and faster, but I didn't stop. If Barnaby had shot Colt, I really had no idea what I was going to do. It wasn't like I had a gun or anything. When I arrived at the house, I half expected to find Colt's lifeless body. Instead, I found Barnaby with a bullet in his leg and Colt standing over him with a gun.

"What happened?" I asked.

"He saw me and came at me. He tried to shoot me, but he missed. I'm a better shot." He handed me the gun. "Hold this on him while I cuff him."

I did as Colt asked. Before Colt even had time to take the gun back, the guys from the county arrived and took over the remainder of the arrest protocol.

"I'm going to be a while," Colt said. "You and Lacy go home. I'll call you later."

"I thought you lost your cell phone."

"I did. I'll call you from the office." He pulled me in toward his body and hugged me tighter than he ever had before. I could hear his heart pounding under my ear. Apparently, he wasn't as unaffected by what went on as he appeared to be.

"I'll go home," I promised. "But don't forget to call."

"I won't. Once I get Barnaby to the hospital, you and I need to have a chat about the inadvisability of putting yourself in a dangerous position when you have no gun and no backup."

"Yeah," I sighed. "I guess I figured that talk was coming."

Chapter 14

"I guess you heard that Rodney went home early," Mylie said to me the following day after I'd arrived on the island, and she'd come over to greet me.

"Georgia mentioned that he'd checked out this morning. I guess his date with Christy yesterday didn't go as planned."

Mylie shook her head. "I spoke to Christy for quite a while this morning. She admitted that Rodney had more than friendship on his mind, and she admitted that she knew it and had let him court her anyway. She told me that she was mad at Noah for choosing his mother over her and wanted to punish him. She also admitted that her need to get back at Noah was childish and that she felt bad about the way the whole thing escalated into something more than it ever should have been."

"So are Noah and Christy okay?"

Mylie paused for a moment and then answered. "I'm not sure. Christy told me that she loves Noah and wants to work things out, but she also shared that she's not willing to get into another relationship where her husband's mother makes decisions that affect her marriage or the way she raises her children. She feels that it's a bad sign that Noah seemed to go back on everything they'd discussed relating to the actual wedding once his mother arrived. Based on what she said, it seems like Noah and Christy have decided to take a step back. They will continue to be friends and even date, but the wedding has been postponed indefinitely."

"I'm sorry to hear that, but it's for the best that all of this came out now. How is Haley doing with everything?"

"She seems fine. Kids are resilient. For the time being, Christy and Haley, and I will continue to share the apartment. That arrangement has been working to this point and will continue to work a while longer. To be honest, I'm hoping Noah and Christy are able to work it out. They seem good for each other. There is this huge issue, but maybe they can find a compromise."

"I hope so. I really do care about both of them." I looked around. "I know they had tickets for today's event. Did they decide to come?"

"No. Noah and Christy both decided to skip it. I think emotions on both sides are pretty raw. But the good news is that Noah, Christy, and Haley decided to babysit Lacy and Lonnie's kids. I guess the twins are no longer contagious, so they not only gave their clam bake tickets to the deserving couple but offered to babysit as well."

I smiled. "That's great. I'm happy it worked out for Lacy and Lonnie to attend. I owe Lacy after almost getting her killed yesterday."

"You almost got her killed?"

I laughed. "It's a long story. I'll tell you about it later. Right now, it looks like Jeremy is waving us over."

Jeremy and Nikki were helping Georgia with the food. It was to the point in the process where they needed help setting everything out on the buffet table. The murder mystery had been played out as everyone enjoyed appetizers and complimentary drinks, and now I could hear the organizers calling everyone to find their seats for the dinner portion of the evening. The same little plastic clams that had been found on the murder victims were being used to deliver the clues, which caused me to feel just a bit queasy, but overall, it seemed that everyone was having a wonderful time.

I noticed a boat pull up just as the group was gathering for the meal. Colt, Lacy, and Lonnie had all arrived. They were too late to join in on the mystery, but just in time to enjoy the food Georgia and Jeremy had prepared.

"I'm so glad you guys could make it." I hugged both Lonnie and Lacy.

"I couldn't believe it when Noah not only offered us his and Christy's tickets but volunteered to babysit as well," Lacy said, grinning.

"It was very nice of both of them, and I'm sure they'll enjoy hanging out with your kids."

Lonnie laughed. "I'm not sure about that, but I wasn't going to say no. Right now, I hear that rum punch Jeremy told me about calling my name."

Both Lonnie and Lacy went in search of a drink while I greeted Colt.

"So, how was your day?" I asked. "Did you wrap things up?"

"Yes, I think things are wrapped up quite nicely."

"Did Barnaby say why he killed four men?"

"Actually, he did. It turns out that his only real target was Oliver Halifax. As Lacy indicated that day in the kitchen when you stopped to speak to her, Barnaby was very much against the proposed project. He honestly felt that if the project was approved, the way of life he loved and greatly valued would forever be destroyed. Barnaby told me that he wasn't too worried about it at first. He figured the town council would never approve such a monstrosity, but then the developer somehow managed to get William Covington on board. He still wasn't worried since the vote would be four to one, but then Ellington Simpleton changed sides, and then it was two to three. Still, three votes against would be enough to send the developer packing, but then Oliver entered the election at the last minute and actually managed to beat Dennis Painter, who was against the project. It was at this point that Barnaby began to understand that the town was really in trouble. When he found out that Oliver not only planned to vote to support that project but that it was very likely he'd cheated to win the seat in the first place, he went a bit crazy. I guess at that point, he began obsessing over the situation, and at some point, he came to the conclusion that Oliver Halifax needed to die."

"So why not just kill him? Why kill the others?"

"Barnaby is the sort to really think things through. He's analytical to a fault. Once the decision was made that Oliver had to die, Barnaby began to plan instead of just killing him. He went through every scenario in his mind time and time again, and at some point, he came to the realization that if he killed Oliver and only Oliver, then all roads would lead back to him. He figured he needed to remove the spotlight from the proposed development as a motive, so he came up with the seven sins thing. I guess he somehow knew that Oliver had attended the weeklong sinners' retreats, and he used that knowledge to come up with a complex plan to get me focused on that week as the motive and not the development."

"Which is exactly what happened," I pointed out.

"Yes, that's exactly what happened."

"Okay, so Barnaby came up with the idea for the note in the clam. But how did that lead to three additional deaths?" I asked.

"Barnaby figured that with just one murder the motive was a moving target, and he didn't want the resort to come into it, so he killed Henry, who he also somehow knew had been to the weeklong men's retreats, and gave him a clam with a similar message. By the time Stan's body showed up, talk about the proposed development as a motive had all but dried up, and everyone was focusing in on the sins these men committed and the company who ran the weeklong retreats."

"I guess his logic did help him come up with a way to get the focus off the development, but why did he kill Kurt? By the time he killed Kurt, everyone was focused on the retreats."

"Barnaby told me that he hadn't planned to kill Kurt, but unfortunately, I managed to catch up with Kurt after I spoke to you last evening. I told him what was going on, hoping that he would use that information to get out of town the way Travis, Don, and Lance had. Of course, Kurt is a hothead, so what he actually did when I left the bar where I'd found him was to go and confront Barnaby. I still don't know how Kurt made the connection between what was going on and Barnaby, but he did. He threatened Barnaby, and Barnaby killed him, and then he left the body with a clam so it would look like his death was simply part of the pattern."

"Wow. I can't believe four men are dead because one man couldn't accept the changes that, while unwelcome by many, still seem inevitable."

"Yeah," Colt sighed. "I really hate to see that project get approved, and now that Oliver is gone, it may not be. Even if Barnaby was ultimately able to stop this great evil as he perceived it to be, he's behind bars and unable to enjoy the town he killed to protect."

I glanced back toward the rows of tables that had been laid out to serve the meal. The theater group was still asking questions of the crowd and going over the clues. It looked like everyone was having a wonderful time.

"It sure has been a long week." I laid my head on Colt's shoulder.

"The longest. I'm glad it's over."

"Are you hungry?"

"Not really. What I really need is a few minutes of peace and quiet. I think I'll go for a walk."

"Do you want company, or would you prefer to go alone? Either is okay with me," I assured him.

"I'd enjoy the company if you feel like you can get away."

"I think Georgia has everything under control."

Colt took my hand in his, and we headed down the beach. We walked in silence for a while, but eventually, he spoke. "I had a nice long conversation with my mother today."

"Oh? How is she doing? How are the kids?"

"Everyone is fine. I've been working on a plan to have the kids with me for three weeks next month, and it looks like it's going to work out. I put in for some time off, and it's been approved. I thought I might take them somewhere for part of the time. Maybe camping. Or Disney World."

"I'm sure they'd enjoy either. I'm glad it worked out for them to come for a visit."

He squeezed my hand. "I'm hoping that you can spend some time with us. I want the three of you to get to know each other better."

"I'd like that. Once you have dates, we can work something out." I knew that Colt had considered having the kids come to live with him once they reached their teens, and while we had most definitely never talked about marriage, I knew that he wanted us all to be a family. I wasn't sure how I felt about that, but I was sure I wanted to get to know two of the people who were among those most important in his life.

"My mom told me that the kids ask about you from time to time."

I raised a brow. "They do? I only met them that one time."

"I guess you made quite an impression. Especially with my niece. My mom is great with them, but I think she misses having a mother."

I think I may have flinched at that point.

"Not that I'm asking you to fill in as her mother," Colt quickly added. "I just think it would be nice for the two of you to have a friendship."

"I'd like that," I said, all the while wondering if I was ready for whatever might be on the horizon with Colt and his niece and nephew. I knew I loved Colt. We never really spoke of love or forever after, but I knew I'd always want him in my life. I also knew that he most likely would become a package deal at some point. Mostly, I'd chosen not to think too far into the future, but the kids were getting older, and if they did come to live with their uncle when they got to a certain age, I supposed that could happen in the not-so-distant future.

I thought about Noah and Christy and how their lack of clear communication may have killed their relationship. I didn't want that for Colt and me, so I supposed, in fairness to both of us, I really should figure out where I stood on moving from couple status to family status.

"I suppose we should get back," I said after we'd walked about as far as you could walk on this small island. "Are you planning to come back to the cottage with me tonight?"

"I'd like that. If it works for you, of course. I'm sure you must be exhausted after spending the whole day preparing for the event."

"I am tired, but I'd like you to come back to the cottage. I'm pretty sure Georgia plans to go home with Tanner, so we'll have the place to ourselves."

Colt stopped walking. He turned my body so that we were facing each other. He slowly lowered his head and kissed me so softly on the lips I could barely feel it. I reached my arms around his neck, pulled him close, and kissed him harder. At that moment, as the moon rose from the east and the sound of laughter could be heard in the distance, I knew in my heart that however a future with Colt might look, it was a future I very much wanted to be part of.

Up Next from Kathi Daley

https://amzn.to/3uflsDL

Continue the adventures of Sydney Whitmore, a forensic psychologist, in a brand new series set on a small island off the coast of California.

After a tragic event Syd decides to head home to Shipwreck Island and the resort owned and operated by her family. As Syd struggles to deal with her loss she also desires a way to help so she renews her relationship with Ezra Reinhold, a reclusive billionaire who enjoys poking around in cold cases and has the means to hire the best people to find the answers no one else has been able to, and she strikes up a working relationship with the island sheriff, Sam Stone.

In book 1 in the series, a group of ten high school students go camping but only eight return. The statements those who've made their way back have told to Sheriff Sam Stone are so different as to be completely useless. Syd has experience getting the truth out of people, as well as helping those who've forgotten to remember, so she agrees to help Sam weed though the data provided to find the truth which both are certain exists beneath the lies.

Meanwhile, Sydney strikes up a friendship with the daughter of a childhood friend who has been the victim of an assault that has left him clinging to life in the hospital; Syd's middle sister Emily has started a new lifestyle blog; her youngest sister Aurora has a new man in her life; and the Miller Family, who've been making the trip to Jack's Hideaway for generations, show up for Aunt Charley's sixtieth birthday party.

https://amzn.to/3spvcd5

The Castaway Bay series is a spinoff of sorts from Summerhouse Reunion, a three part story which published last summer. It is not necessary to have read Summerhouse Reunion to enjoy Castaway Bay but if you would like to have the history of some of the characters including Sydney's friend Kelly Green, Rory's boss Ryder Westlake, and Sheriff Sam Stone, it might be a good idea to read the complete story before you begin.

Up Next from Holiday Bay

https://amzn.to/3stnm28

Abby is offered the chance to participate in an author event being held at Firehouse Books with one of her own favorite authors. When the guest author turns up dead, Abby realizes that clues to the author's death could be found in the new novel the woman had yet to release. Using her own sleuthing skills, Abby jumps into the investigation after it becomes clear that it just might take an author to find the meaning in the pages.

Meanwhile it is weeks before Halloween and the inn is filled with guests looking for a spooky weekend retreat. Join Abby, Georgia, Jeremy, Nikki, and Mylie as they host a series of events designed to provide thrills and chills to all who dare to venture within.

USA Today best-selling author Kathi Daley lives in beautiful Lake Tahoe with her husband, Ken. When she isn't writing, she likes spending time hiking the miles of desolate trails surrounding her home. Find out more about her books at www.kathidaley.com

Made in the USA
Las Vegas, NV
08 December 2021